凝煉知識品味閱讀

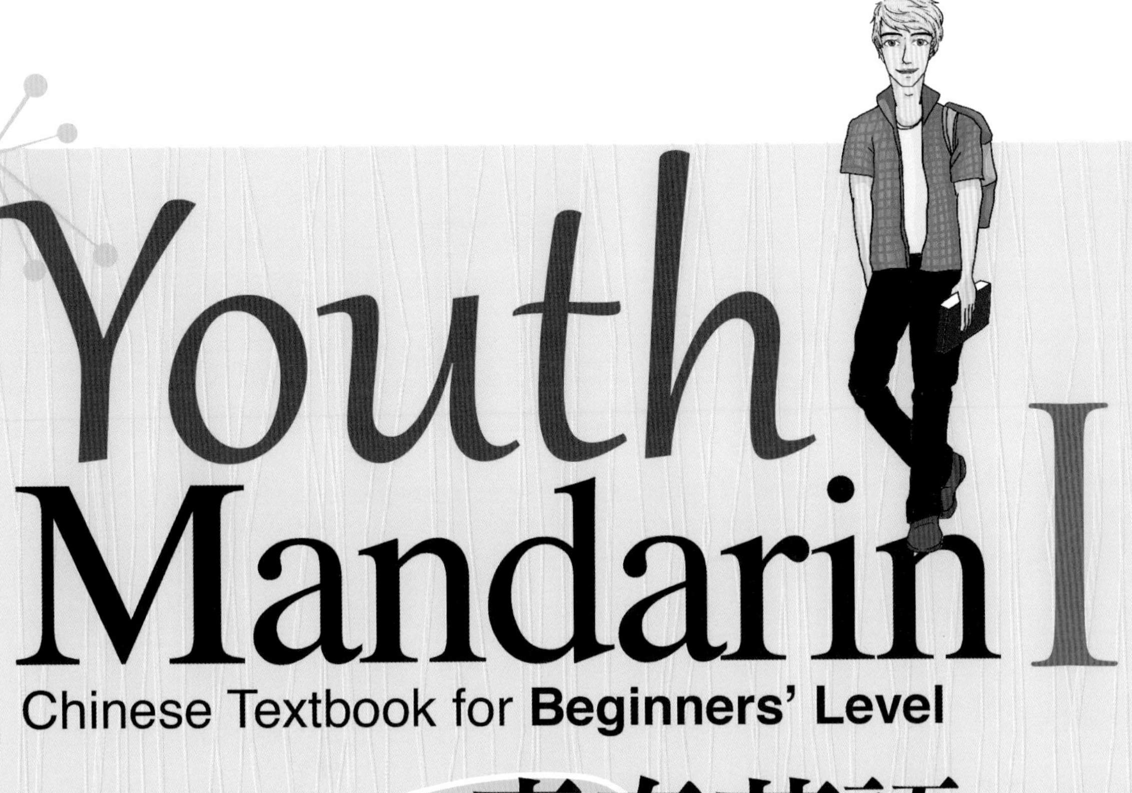

Youth Mandarin I

Chinese Textbook for **Beginners' Level**

青春華語（一）

Editor-in-chief
Shih-chang Hsin
Editors
Huai-xuan Chen
Chu-hua Huang
Yu-hui Huang

Preface

A. Introducing the Book

1. Target reader: beginners in junior and senior high school.
2. Duration: one semester, suitable for the schools with less Chinese learning hours.
3. The texts come in both traditional and simplified Chinese. Pinyin is also included. A glossary is attached at the end of the book.
4. Chinese characters: 276 different Chinese characters are included.
5. Vocabulary: 286 words (meaning units) are included.
6. Sentence patterns: 56 sentence patterns are included.

B. Structure and Concepts

There are 12 units in this book and each unit starts with warm-up activities to engage the students. Following are the three major sections of a unit: core activities, after-class practice and exercise, and supplementary materials.

1. Core Activities

There are two lessons in one unit. Each lesson includes a story, a dialogue, discussions, vocabulary, expressions, and grammar.

(1) Story: the story is written in English so as to help the learner understand the context of the dialogue that follows.

(2) Dialogue: readers can learn different speech styles from the characters for their backgrounds, genders, and personalities differ.

(3) Discussions: discussions help students understand the content and meaning of the dialogue.

(4) Vocabulary and expressions: new words are those that show up

in the book for the first time and expressions are set phrases such as: 怎麼了？and 太棒了！We put vocabulary and expressions into separate sheets so the teachers can apply different teaching methods when leading practice sessions.

(5) Grammar: emphasizing on sentence patterns; useful sentence patterns are provided.

2. After-class Practice and Exercise

After-class practice and exercise come after core activities and consist of grammar practice and application.

(1) Grammar practice: have the students repeatedly practice sentence structures until they become innate.

(2) Application: applying what has been learned by completing a dialogue in the given scenario or completing related tasks.

3. Supplementary Materials

Supplementary explanation and culture note are provided at the end of every unit.

(1) Supplementary explanation: explaining some language nuances that need to be paid attention to or listing out some supplementary words.

(2) Culture note: notes on sceneries and historical sites, festivals and customs, taboos, dining culture, and etc. are provided in accordance with the topic of each unit.

The textbook is developed by the Videoconferencing Chinese Team (VC Chinese). VC Chinese is a research team formed by professors and graduate assistants for instructional materials development and teacher training for distance Chinese teaching.

——VC Chinese Team

編輯前言

A. 教材簡介

1.使用對象：本教材是針對初、高中年齡層的華語初學者所編寫。

2.教學時間：可使用一個學期，適於每週中文課時數較少的學校使用。

3.課文均有繁體字、簡體字及漢語拼音。課本最後附有全冊的生詞表。

4.漢字量：本教材共有276不同的漢字。

5.生詞量：本教材共有286個詞。

6.句型量：本教材共有56個中文句型。

B. 教材結構及編寫理念

本教材共有12個單元（Unit），每個單元首先以暖身活動引起學習動機。再分爲三大部分：教學核心活動、課後練習活動、課外補充材料。

1.教學核心活動

各單元之下有兩課：每課包括故事情節、對話、討論、生詞、固定說法及語法，此爲教學核心部分。

⑴故事情節：先以英文敘述故事情節，讓學習者進入眞實情境，了解語言實際使用的場景。

⑵對話：透過不同背景、性別、個性的人物展開對話，藉以顯現不同人物，語言使用的風格也有所不同，同時也是學習者學習模仿的語言形式。

⑶討論：經過問題討論，確認學習者了解對話的內容及含意。

⑷詞彙及固定說法：詞彙爲學習者首次學習的詞彙，而固定說法則是一些常用習慣語，如：「怎麼了？」「太棒了！」，我們

希望將這些習慣用語和生詞做切分，以便老師在練習時可採用不同練習方式。

⑸語法：主要以句型爲主，強調功能實用性。

2.課後練習活動

教學核心活動結束之後，進行課後練習，分爲語法操練和應用練習。

⑴語法操練：以語法句型機械式操練爲主，在於鞏固形式，強調熟練性。

⑵應用練習：以完成情境對話及任務活動方式，眞實運用所學。

3.課外補充材料

每單元結束後，提供與單元主題相關之語言及文化知識。

⑴語言補充：說明一些語言形式使用注意事項，或補充相關詞彙。

⑵文化知識：根據各單元主題，補充相關的文化知識，包括介紹風景名勝、節慶習俗、生活禁忌、餐飲習慣等。

——VC Chinese Team

Topic Function & Language Skill

各單元主題功能和語言技能

UNIT	SUBJECT	TOPIC	LANGUAGE SKILL
UNIT 1	I am your student.	Person, possessive	Saying Hello & Greetings
UNIT 2	Your Mandarin is very good.	Ability	Introduce Yourself & Praise
UNIT 3	How many people are there in your family?	Appellation, Number	Introduce Your Family & Title
UNIT 4	Please come over to my house.	Days of the Week	Invitation
UNIT 5	What day is your birthday?	Date & Age	Inquiry
UNIT 6	How do you get to the Chinese supermarket?	Direction & Location	Asking for directions
UNIT 7	Let's have some Chinese Food.	Food, Flavors	Recommending
UNIT 8	Your photos are interesting!	Adjective	Descriptions & Requests
UNIT 9	What color do you like?	Colors	Shopping
UNIT 10	What happened to Linda?	Body parts & Symptoms	Asking for Leave & Showing Concerns
UNIT 11	The Weather in New York	Weather & Transportation	Comparison
UNIT 12	Where are you going for your vacation?	Making plans	Proposal & Acceptance

Grammar & Cultural Notes

文法和文化點

Unit	Lesson	Grammar	Cultural Note
1	1	personal pronoun + 是 + name/title Someone + 的 + N	1. Chinese Family Name （中國百家姓） 2. Greeting gestures in China and America （東西方打招呼的手勢） 3. Have You Eaten Yet? （吃飽了沒？）
	2	personal pronoun + 叫 + Name	
2	1	someone + 會 + V N + 很 + Adj N + 也 + V	1. Chinese Martial Arts （中國功夫） 2. Modesty in Chinese Culture （華人的謙虛觀念）
	2	這 + 是 + N	
3	1	1. Someone 有 N 2. Number measure word N 3. 這 NumberMeasure Word	1. Three Generations Living Under One Roof 華人社會中的三代同堂 2. Chinese Immigration in the U.S. 美國社會的華人移民轉變
	2	1. N. + 是哪裡人？ 2. Someone 在 place word	
4	1	1. Someonea specific timeV 2. Someone請 + someone V	1. Origin of the Mid-Autumn Festival 華人的中秋節及由來 2. Food on Chinese Holidays 中國特別的節慶食物
	2	1. Someone + 可以V + 嗎(ma) 2. 一起Verb	
5	1	…是什麼時候？ Certain holiday or special day + 是…月…日	1. Celebrating Birthdays in China 中國人的慶生方式 2. Chinese Zodiac 中國的生肖
	2	1. ...，S + 呢？	
6	1	1. 到some place怎麼走？ 2. N在哪兒？ 3. Noun在Some place 4. Someone往 + direction走	1. Origin of the Chinatown 美國唐人街的由來 2. Differences in Western and Eastern Chinese Children 深植於美國的社會服務觀念——美國華裔與亞洲孩子的不同 3. Tiger Mother 虎媽對美國社會的震盪
	2	1. Something在哪裡？ 2. N裡面 + 有N2	

<table>
<tr><th>Unit</th><th>Lesson</th><th>Grammar</th><th>Cultural Note</th></tr>
<tr><td rowspan="2">7</td><td>1</td><td>1. 哪 + Measure word Noun SV？
2. So I have heard that⋯
3. V過 N</td><td rowspan="2">1. Delicious Chinese food
美味中國菜
2. Chopsticks
筷子</td></tr>
<tr><td>2</td><td>1. ⋯，像(such as)⋯
2. maybeScan Verb (give a suggestion)</td></tr>
<tr><td rowspan="2">8</td><td>1</td><td>1. N看起來 + SV
2. V了N</td><td rowspan="2">1. Social Network
社群網路
2. Yin Yang in Chinese Dishes
陰陽與中國菜</td></tr>
<tr><td>2</td><td>1. Someone可以 + V + N + 嗎？
2. 有一點兒 + SV</td></tr>
<tr><td rowspan="2">9</td><td>1</td><td>1. 哪 + numbermeasure word
2. Noun 比較SV
3. V + 的時候
4. 最好 + V</td><td rowspan="2">1. Cultural Colors
不同文化的顏色內涵
2. Evolution of Chinese Fashion
華人服裝的變遷</td></tr>
<tr><td>2</td><td>1. 有沒有 + Number/大中小 + 號 + Noun
2. N1 + N2 + (someone) + 都 + V
3. 請 + 給someone number Measure word + N
4. Verbsame Verb看</td></tr>
<tr><td rowspan="2">10</td><td>1</td><td>1. Someone V了</td><td rowspan="2">1. Traditional Chinese Medicine-acupuncture & massage
中國的傳統醫學療法—針灸與推拿
2. Dietary Therapy
藥食同源：中國人的食補觀念</td></tr>
<tr><td>2</td><td>1. 不Verb了
2. 好像 V 了
3. Someone要 + 多Verb</td></tr>
<tr><td rowspan="2">11</td><td>1</td><td>1. Noun跟Noun + 一樣SV
2. Noun + 比 + Noun SV + 得SV</td><td rowspan="2">1. Umbrellas On Sunny Days
晴天雨天都撐傘的中國人
2. Test Culture
亞洲國家的升學制度</td></tr>
<tr><td>2</td><td>1. Someone平常 + Verb
2. 有的 候Verb
3. Someone常常/很少Verb</td></tr>
<tr><td rowspan="2">12</td><td>1</td><td>1. 快要Verb了
2. 人 + 跟 + 人Verb
3. 讓someone Verb 一下</td><td rowspan="2">1. New Year's Eve in Asia
亞洲地區的跨年及慶祝活動
2. Chinese New Year
中國新年
3. Public Holidays
國定假日</td></tr>
<tr><td>2</td><td>1. Someone maybeV
2. Someone Verb tosomeone</td></tr>
</table>

Abbreviation

詞性簡表

Abbreviation	Case	Chinese
Adv	Adverb	副詞
AV	Auxiliary Verb	助動詞
MW	Measure Word	量詞
N	Noun	名詞
NU	Number	數字
PW	Place Word	地方詞
P	Particle	助詞
QW	Question Word	疑問詞
Adj / SV	Adjective / Stative Verb	形容詞 / 狀態動詞
TW	Time Word	時間詞
V	Verb	動詞
Pro	Pronoun	代名詞
Prep	Preposition	介詞
Conj	Conjunction	連接詞

Story

The fall semester will start soon. This year, Mark, Lin, Linda, Maria, Jennifer, and Jeff will become 10th grade students.

Mark and Lin are good friends. They are also teammates on the school basketball team. This year, their goal is to win the championship in high school basketball tournament. Linda and Maria are cheerleaders. They cheer for the basketball team very often.

Jennifer and Jeff are the president and vice president of the Kung Fu Club. Jennifer is practicing for the youth kung fu tournament. Jeff loves kung fu and many different aspects of Chinese culture.

There are two levels of Chinese classes this semester, basic level and intermediate level. Mark, Linda, and Maria are placed in the basic level class taught by teacher Daisy.

Characters

Mark was born in Boston. He loves sports, especially basketball. He is currently the captain of the high school basketball team. He likes his friends and is a very popular guy at school. His father works in an international trading company at New York and his mother is a housewife. His younger brother, Henry, is an 8th grade student at the same high school.

Lin moved to the States with his family when he was six years old. He has a sister, Wendy, and a brother, Lucas. He lives only a few blocks away from Mark, so they get together to play basketball every once in a while. Lin speaks Mandarin at home with his parents but his reading and writing abilities are not as good. His parents are encouraging him to take more Mandarin courses. Lin will take an intermediate level Mandarin class this semester.

Linda is an African American student. Her father is a policeman and her mother is a nurse. Linda has two sisters, Ginny and Laura. Linda's hobby is painting. She wants to become a fashion designer in the future. Linda is a cheerleader of the basketball team. Her best friend is Maria.

Maria's parents moved to the States from Mexico when she was very young. She speaks both Spanish and English. Her hobbies are cooking and dancing. She loves Chinese food, especially the spicy Sichuan cuisine. She has a brother named Dominic and her sister is Olivia. Maria is also a cheerleader.

Jennifer's mom came from Shanghai. She speaks Mandarin with her mother at home. Jennifer's parents worked as computer engineers at Silicon Valley of California, and moved to New York just a couple of years ago. Jennifer started practicing martial arts when she was very young and has won several medals. Jennifer is not only passionate about martial arts, but also enjoys the great time she has with her masters and kung fu buddies. This semester, Jennifer will be a 10th grade student and she will also be the head of the kung fu club. Jennifer has a brother named Kevin.

Jeff's mother is a primary school teacher. He has been fascinated by Chinese kung fu ever since he was a kid. He is also interested in Chinese culture, especially Chinese chess and calligraphy. Chinese characters sometimes look like drawings or paintings to him. He took some Mandarin courses before and got good grades. This semester, he will take the intermediate level Mandarin course. His biggest dream is to travel to China in the future. Jeff is currently the vice-president of Kung Fu Club.

Contents

Contents

I am your student.

我是你的學生

Warm Up Activities

1. Do you know what your teacher's Chinese name is?
2. In your country, do you use gestures when saying Hello?

LESSON 1

STORY

This is the first day of semester. Mark is sitting in the classroom, quite exited for the first day of class. The teacher for the basic level Mandarin course is Ms. Lee. Ms. Lee walks into the classroom when the bell rings and introduces herself to the students.

DIALOGUE

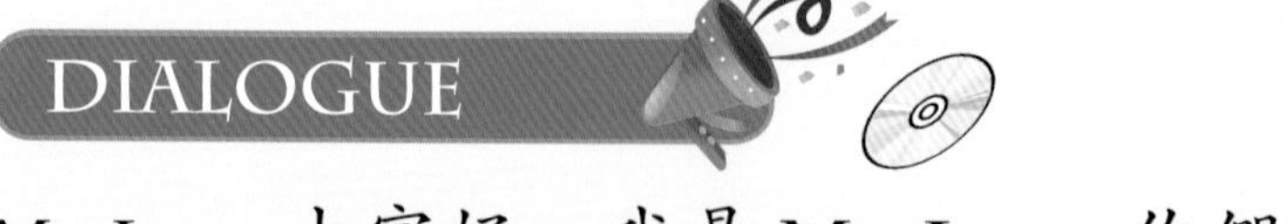

Ms. Lee：大家好。我是 Ms. Lee，你們的中文老師。
大家好。我是 Ms. Lee，你们的中文老师。
Dàjiāhǎo。Wǒ shì Ms. Lee，nǐmen de Zhōngwén lǎoshī。

Mark：你好。我是 Mark，你的學生。
你好。我是 Mark，你的学生。
Nǐhǎo。Wǒ shì Mark，nǐ de xuéshēng。

Maria：我們是你的學生。
我们是你的学生。
Wǒmen shì nǐ de xuéshēng。

Ms. Lee：你們好。
你们好。
Nǐmenhǎo。

Ms. Lee: Hello everyone. I am Ms. Lee. I am your Mandarin teacher.
Mark: Hello, I am Mark. I am your student.
Maria: We are your students.
Ms. Lee: Hi you guys.

DISCUSSION

Who are Ms. Lee's students?

VOCABULARY

	Traditional Characters	Simplified Characters	Pinyin	English
1	我ㄨㄛˇ	我	wǒ	(P) I
2	我ㄨㄛˇ們˙ㄇㄣ	我们	wǒmen	(P) we
3	是ㄕˋ	是	shì	(V) to be
4	你ㄋㄧˇ（妳ㄋㄧˇ）	你（妳）	nǐ(nǐ)	(P) you (singular)
5	你ㄋㄧˇ們˙ㄇㄣ	你们	nǐmen	(P) you (plural)
6	的˙ㄉㄜ	的	de	(possessive or modifying particle)
7	中ㄓㄨㄥ文ㄨㄣˊ	中文	zhōngwén	(N) Mandarin
8	老ㄌㄠˇ師ㄕ	老师	lǎoshī	(N) teacher
9	學ㄒㄩㄝˊ生ㄕㄥ	学生	xuéshēng	(N) student

EXPRESSION

	Traditional Characters	Simplified Characters	Pinyin	English
1	大家好	大家好	dàjiāhăo	hi, everyone
2	大家	大家	dàjiā	everyone
3	你好	你好	nĭhăo	hi; Hello
4	你們好	你们好	nĭmenhăo	hi; Hello

GRAMMAR

1. personal pronoun + 是 + name/title
personal pronoun + shì + name/title

Examples:

我是學生。

我是学生。

Wǒ shì xuéshēng。

I am a student.

2. someone + 的 + N
someone + de + N

Examples:

你們的老師。

你们的老师。

Nǐmen de lǎoshī。

Your teacher.

你的學生。

你的学生。

Nǐ de xuéshēng。

Your student.

LESSON 2

STORY

Linda and Maria are also taking the basic level Mandarin class. They are cheerleaders and they cheer for Mark and the basketball team at basketball games. Linda and Maria are happy that they are taking the same Mandarin class with Mark. Today in class, Ms. Lee asks the students to introduce themselves to each other in Mandarin.

DIALOGUE

Mark：我是 Mark。你叫什麼名字？
我是 Mark。你叫什么名字?
Wǒ shì Mark。Nǐ jiào shénme míngzì ？

Maria：我叫 Maria。
我叫 Maria。
Wǒ jiào Maria。

Ms. Lee：很好，Maria。（points to Linda）她是誰？
很好，Maria。（points to Linda）她是谁？
Hěnhǎo，Maria。（points to Linda）Tā shì shéi ？

Maria：她是 Linda。她是我的朋友。
她是 Linda。她是我的朋友。
Tā shì Linda。Tā shì wǒ de péngyǒu。

Mark: I am Mark. What is your name?
Maria: I am Maria.
Ms. Lee: Very good, Maria. Who is she?
Maria: She is Linda. She is my friend.

DISCUSSION

1. What are the names of Ms. Lee's students?
2. Who is Maria's friend?

VOCABULARY

	Traditional Characters	Simplified Characters	Pinyin	English
1	叫ㄐㄧㄠˋ	叫	jiào	(V) to call
2	什ㄕㄜˊ麼˙ㄇㄜ	什么	shénme	(Pro) what
3	名ㄇㄧㄥˊ字ㄗˋ	名字	míngzì	(N) name
4	很ㄏㄣˇ	很	hěn	(Adv) very
5	好ㄏㄠˇ	好	hǎo	(Adj) good
6	他ㄊㄚ（她ㄊㄚ）	他（她）	tā / tā	(Pro) he/she
7	誰ㄕㄟˊ	谁	shéi	(Pro) who
8	朋ㄆㄥˊ友ㄧㄡˇ	朋友	péngyǒu	(N) friend

GRAMMAR

personal pronoun + 叫 + Name

personal pronoun + jiào + Name

Examples:

我叫 Mark。

我叫 Mark。

Wǒ jiào Mark。

I am called Mark. (My name is Mark.)

我叫 Maria。

我叫 Maria。

Wǒ jiào Maria。

I am called Maria. (My name is Maria.)

I. PRACTICE

1. 什麼 什么 shénme (Interrogative Pronoun- what)

The question sentences formed by "what, who, where, which, and when" do not start with these interrogative pronouns. In Chinese, the interrogative pronouns are placed where you would place the object in a positive sentence.

Q：妳叫什麼名字？
你叫什么名字?
Nǐ jiào shénme míngzì ？
You are called (by) what name? (What is your name?)

A：我叫 Maria。
我叫 Maria。
Wǒ jiào Maria。
I am (called) Maria.

Practice

Q：你叫什麼名字？
你叫什么名字？
Nǐ jiào shénme míngzi ？
What is your name? (You are called (by) what name?)
A：________________。

2. 誰 谁 shéi (Interrogative Pronoun-who)

Q：她是誰？
她是谁？
Tā shì shéi ？
Who is she?

A：她是 Linda。她是我的朋友。

她是 Linda。她是我的朋友。

Tā shì Linda。Tā shì wǒ de péngyǒu。

She is Linda. She is my friend.

Practice

Q：你是誰？

你是谁？

Nǐ shì shéi ？

Who are you?

A：________________。

II. EXERCISE

1. Complete the following dialogues:

A：__________？

B：我叫__________。

Wǒ jiào __________。

A：__________？

B：我是__________。

Wǒ shì __________。

2. Complete the following task:

Ask your classmates what their Chinese names are and make a list.

III. SUPPLEMENTARY EXPLANATIONS

1. Chinese names start with the last name and the first name is placed after the last name.
2. Some Chinese words that start with the character " 老 lǎo" do not necessarily carry the meaning of "being old."

Examples:

老師
老师
lǎoshī
means teacher.

老鼠
老鼠
lǎoshǔ
means rats.

IV. CULTURAL NOTES

1. Chinese Family Name（中國百家姓）

Personal introductions between westerners and Chinese people can be slightly confusing. That's because China and the West are different when it comes to the order of one's full name. In China, one's family name appears at the beginning, whereas one's given name comes after. In this way, "John Smith" would actually be known as "Smith John" in Chinese. Chinese family names are typically one Chinese character, although some family names are two. Given names can either be one or two characters. Sometimes one's full name has a total of four characters, but this is much more common in Japan than it is in China.

So where did Chinese family names come from? There are thousands of family names that have been past down over the course of history, and many are more than 2500 years old. Today, there are still over 6000 family names used in Chinese society, but only several hundred are commonly used. Some of the most common family names include: 張 (Zhāng), 李 (Lǐ), and 王 (Wáng). In fact, there are over 100 million Chinese people with the last name Zhang! Many Chinese families have family trees that can trace their ancestors back thousands of years.

One's given name in Chinese culture is often filled with very deep meaning, not only because of the way a name might sound in Chinese, but also because it reflects the hopes and dreams that parents have for their children. Although one can often tell if someone is male or female by reading their full name, this is not always the case, which can lead to some embarrassment and confusion during the first encounter.

2.Greeting gestures in China and America（東西方打招呼的手勢）

Greeting gestures in Chinese and American culture are not quite the same. Generally speaking, Chinese people would wave, shake hands, nod, or do a slight bow, but never do they get into physical contact such as giving hugs or kisses on the cheeks. Chinese people would do an exchange of minor bows or slight nods to greet others and to whom they bow to reflect the culture's concept of social status. Students would bow to their teachers, juniors would bow to their seniors, and subordinates would bow to their bosses. Handshaking is another common way of greeting others, especially when meeting for the first time. When greeting friends or familiar faces, waving is more common.

When greeting others in traditional Chinese culture, the right hand grabs the left hand and shakes back and forth by the chin. This greeting style exhibits the reserved style of traditional Chinese culture. Although this style is rarely seen today, it can still be seen in kungfu movies.

3.Have You Eaten Yet?（吃飽了沒？）

Living in China or Taiwan you might be quite surprised the first time someone asks you "吃了嗎？ chī le ma?" or "吃飽了沒？ chī bǎo le méi ？". While these expressions translate to "Have you eaten?" and "Are you full?" the person asking isn't as interested in what you just had for lunch as they are in simply saying "hello." This interesting greeting has its roots in China's past when families didn't always have a lot to eat, and therefore, it was polite to ask others if they have eaten or not, especially during meal times. Today this greeting is similar to asking in English, “What’s up?” or “How’s it going?” as polite small talk and nothing more. As to how to respond to such a greeting, it’s best to say “ 吃了。chī le,” which means “I’ve eaten” even if your stomach is growling!

第二章 UNIT 2

Your Mandarin is very good.

你的中文很好

Warm Up Activities

1. What aspects of Chinese language and Chinese culture interest you the most?
2. In your daily life, what opportunities do you have to get in touch with Chinese culture?

LESSON 1

STORY

Mark ran into Lin in the hallway during the break between classes. A poster of activities held by the Chinese Kungfu club attracted their attention and they decided to check out this club. After classes, Mark and Lin went to the Kungfu Club and Lin saw Jeff, an old classmate, there. After Jeff introduced them to Jennifer, the club president, Jennifer started demonstrating some basic movements of Taiji. When Jennifer finished the demonstration, she speaks to Mark and Lin in fluent Mandarin, which surprised Mark.

DIALOGUE

Jennifer：我是Jennifer，功夫社的社長。你們會說中文嗎？
我是 Jennifer，功夫社的社长。你们会说中文吗？
Wǒ shì Jennifer，Gōngfūshè de shèzhǎng。Nǐmen huì shuō Zhōngwén ma?

Mark：我是 Mark，他是 Lin。他會說中文，他的中文很好。
我是 Mark，他是 Lin。他会说中文，他的中文很好。
Wǒ shì Mark，tā shì Lin。Tā huì shuō Zhōngwén，tā de Zhōngwén hěn hǎo。

Lin：Jennifer，你的中文也不錯。
Jennifer，你的中文也不错。
Jennifer，nǐ de Zhōngwén yě búcuò。

Jennifer：謝謝。歡迎你們。
谢谢。欢迎你们。
Xièxie。Huānyíng nǐmen。

Jennifer: I am Jennifer, the president of the Kungfu Club. Do you speak Mandarin?
Mark: I am Mark. He is Lin. He can speak Mandarin. His Mandarin is very good.
Lin: Jennifer, your Mandarin is also not bad.
Jennifer: Thank you. Welcome to the Kungfu club.

DISCUSSION

1. Who is the president of the Kungfu club?
2. Who can speak Mandarin?

VOCABULARY

	Traditional Characters	Simplified Characters	Pinyin	English
1	社長	社长	shèzhǎng	(N)president/director
2	社	社	shè	club
3	會	会	huì	(Av)be able to
4	說	说	shuō	(V)speak
5	也	也	yě	(Adv)also

TERM

	Traditional Characters	Simplified Characters	Pinyin	English
1	功夫	功夫	gōngfū	(N) Chinese Kungfu

EXPRESSION

	Traditional Characters	Simplified Characters	Pinyin	English
1	不錯	不错	búcuò	not bad
2	謝謝	谢谢	xièxie	thank you
3	歡迎	欢迎	huānyíng	welcome

GRAMMAR

1. Someone + 會 + V
Someone + huì + V

Example:

Lin 會說中文。

Lin 会说中文。

Lin huì shuō Zhōngwén。

Lin can speak Mandarin.

2. N + 很 + Adj
N + hěn + Adj

Example:

Jennifer 的中文很不錯。

Jennifer 的中文很不错。

Jennifer de Zhōngwén hěn búcuò。

Jennifer's Mandarin is very good (not bad).

3. N + 也 + V
N +yě + V

Example:

Lin 的中文很好，Mark 的中文也不錯。

Lin 的中文很好，Mark 的中文也不错。

Lin de Zhōngwén hěn hǎo，Mark de Zhōngwén yě búcuò。

Lin's Mandarin is very good. Mark's Mandarin is also very good.

LESSON 2

STORY

Lin and Jeff are both students in the intermediate level Mandarin class but they do not know each other very well. For Lin, Jeff seems to be a quiet and hardworking student. Today, Lin introduces Jeff to his friend, Mark.

DIALOGUE

Lin：Mark，這是我中級班的同學，Jeff。
Mark，这是我中级班的同学，Jeff。
Mark，zhè shì wǒ zhōngjí bān de tóngxué，Jeff。

Mark：你好，我是 Mark。
你好，我是 Mark。
Nǐhǎo，wǒ shì Mark。

Lin：Jeff，你的中文很好。
Jeff，你的中文很好。
Jeff，nǐ de Zhōngwén hěn hǎo。

Jeff：哪裡，哪裡。我喜歡說中文。
哪里，哪里。我喜欢说中文。
Nǎlǐ，nǎlǐ。Wǒ xǐhuān shuō Zhōngwén。

Mark：很高興認識你。
很高兴认识你。
Hěn gāoxìng rènshì nǐ。

Lin: Mark, this is Jeff, my classmate in the intermediate Mandarin class.
Mark: Hi, I am Mark.
Lin: Jeff, your Chinese is very good.
Jeff: Thank you! I like to speak Mandarin.
Mark: Glad to meet you.

DISCUSSION

1. Who is Jeff?
2. Can Jeff speak Mandarin?

VOCABULARY

	Traditional Characters	Simplified Characters	Pinyin	English
1	這	这	zhè	(Pro) this
2	中級	中级	zhōngjí	(Adj) intermediate level
3	班	班	bān	(N) class
4	同學	同学	tóngxué	(N) classmate
5	喜歡	喜欢	xǐhuān	(V) to like
6	高興	高兴	gāoxìng	(Adj) glad
7	認識	认识	rènshì	(V) to meet, to get to know

EXPRESSION

	Traditional Characters	Simplified Characters	Pinyin	English
1	哪ㄋㄚˇ裡ㄌㄧˇ	哪里	nǎlǐ	a humble expression to respond to a praise
2	很ㄏㄣˇ高ㄍㄠ興ㄒㄧㄥˋ認ㄖㄣˋ識ㄕˋ你ㄋㄧˇ	很高兴认识你	Hěn gāoxìng rènshì nǐ	glad to meet you

GRAMMAR

這 + 是 + N

Zhè + shì + N

This + be + N

Example:

這是我的同學 Lin。

这是我的同学 Lin。

Zhè shì wǒ de tóngxué Lin。

This is my classmate, Lin.

I. PRACTICE

1. 會（huì）

Q：你會說中文嗎？

你会说中文吗？

Nǐ huì shuō Zhōngwén ma ？

Can you speak Mandarin?

A：我不會說中文。

我不会说中文。

Wǒ bú huì shuō Zhōngwén。

I can not speak Mandarin.

Practice

Q：你會不會說中文？

你会不会说中文？

Nǐ huìbúhuì shuō Zhōngwén ？

Can you speak Mandarin?

A：________________。

2. 好（hǎo）

Q：你的中文好不好？

你的中文好不好？

Nǐ de Zhōngwén hǎobùhǎo ？

How is your Mandarin?

A：我的中文很好。

我的中文很好。

Wǒ de Zhōngwén hěn hǎo。

My Mandarin is very good.

Practice

Q：你的功夫好嗎？

你的功夫好吗？

Nǐ de Gōngfū hǎo ma ？

How is your kungfu?

A：________________。

II. EXERCISE

1. Complete the following dialogues:

A：__________?

B：我不會中國功夫。

我不会中国功夫。

Wǒ búhuì Zhōngguó Gōngfū。

A：你的中文好嗎？

你的中文好吗？

Nǐ de Zhōngwén hǎo ma ？

B：________。

2. Tasks

(1) Introduce the classmate sitting next to you to other students.

(2) Ask your classmates what languages they can speak and what language they use and home and then make a list.

III. SUPPLEMENTARY EXPLANATION

1. The term "中文 Zhōngwén" is a general term that stands for all languages and dialects used by 56 ethnic groups in China. Among these languages, Mandarin (官话 guānhuà) is the representative language used by Han people, the largest ethnic group in China. Therefore, it is called "漢語 汉语 Hànyǔ"(the language of Han) in China. Because it is the most widely used language in China, it is also called "普通話 普通话 pǔtōnghuà". In Taiwan, Mandarin is referred to as "國語 国语 Guóyǔ" domestically and "華語 华语 Huáyǔ" internationally. Nowadays, "中 文 Zhōngwén" usually refers to Mandarin in the field of language instruction or in most occasions.
2. When one is complimented by others, a polite form is to say "哪裡，哪裡 Nǎlǐ nǎlǐ" as a response. Recently, more and more Chinese people are willing to accept other's compliments by saying "謝謝 谢谢 Xièxie" (Thank you.)

IV. CULTURAL NOTES

1. Chinese Martial Arts（中國功夫）

Chinese martial arts is popularly known as " 功夫 Gōngfū" or " 武術 Wǔ shù" can be seen in many movies such as Crouching Tiger Hidden Dragon or Kungfu Panda. Famous practitioners of Chinese martial arts include Jet Li and Jackie Chan.

The term " 功夫 " ('gōng' meaning "work, energy or achievement" and 'fū' meaning "man or intensity") is referred to Chinese martial arts, but also means skill cultivated through hard work. " 武術 Wǔshù" literally means "martial arts" in Chinese.

Chinese martial arts is inspired by Chinese philosophies, religions and legends. It is famous for its animal styles such as eagle claw, praying mantis, snake, monkey, white crane, tiger, etc. Many of its routines incorporate weapons such as straightsword, broadsword, staff, spear, daggers, pudao, and many more.

There are many ways to classify Chinese martial arts. One way is to categorize it into two main styles: internal and external. Internal style focuses on " 氣 Qì" manipulation, such as " 太 極 Tàijí", and external style concentrates on improving muscle and cardiovascular fitness. Another method of classifying Chinese martial arts is based on geographical association: "northern" and southern" style. Northern style focuses on extended movements and requires the use of force for quick fluid transitions. Southern style, on the other hand, focuses on low stable stances and short powerful movements for attack.

2. Modesty in Chinese Culture（華人的謙虛觀念）

Modesty or 謙虛 qiānxū is a traditional virtue of Chinese culture, stemming from the great scholar Confucius. To Confucius, modesty and humility are qualities that a society needs in order to sustain and flourish. Modesty may come in the form of a host apologizing for a "small quantity" or an "ill-prepared" meal that is served to guests, which is almost always far from the truth. Another common and everyday example of modesty is responding to a compliment by saying, "哪裡，哪裡 nǎlǐ, nálǐ", literally "where, where" which figuratively means "I have done nothing to deserve your compliment."

So the next time someone tells you how good your Chinese sounds, ask yourself: "What would Confucius say?"

第三章 UNIT 3

How many people are there in your family?

你家有幾個人？

Warm Up Activities

1. How do you and your family members share household chores?
2. Do you have any brothers or sisters?

LESSON 1

STORY

Today the students in the basic level Mandarin class have to introduce their family members by bringing in photos or showing them on powerpoint. Linda pulls out the photos that she posted on the internet and starts to introduce her family members.

DIALOGUE

Ms. Lee：Linda，你家有幾個人？
Linda，你家有几个人？
Linda，nǐjiā yǒu jǐgerén ？

Linda：我家有五個人。
我家有五个人。
Wǒjiā yǒu wǔ ge rén。

Ms. Lee：他們是誰？
他们是谁？
Tāmen shì shéi ？

Linda：這是我爸爸、媽媽。這兩個是我妹妹。
这是我爸爸、妈妈。这两个是我妹妹。
Zhè shì wǒ bàba、māma。Zhè liǎng ge shì wǒ mèimei。

Ms. Lee：你的妹妹都很可愛。
你的妹妹都很可爱。
Nǐ de mèimei dōu hěn kěài。

> Ms. Lee: Linda, how many people are there in your family?
> Linda: There are five people in my family.
> Ms. Lee: Who are they?
> Linda: This is my father and mother. These are my younger sisters.
> Ms. Lee: Your younger sisters are very pretty.

DISCUSSION

1. How many people are there in Linda's family?
2. Who are they?

VOCABULARY

	Traditional Characters	Simplified Characters	Pinyin	English
1	家ㄐㄧㄚ	家	jiā	(N) family
2	有ㄧㄡˇ	有	yǒu	(V) There are...; to have
3	幾ㄐㄧˇ	几	jǐ	(Pro) how many
4	個˙ㄍㄜ	个	ge	measure word
5	五ㄨˇ	五	wǔ	(NU) five
6	爸ㄅㄚˋ爸˙ㄅㄚ	爸爸	bàba	(N) father
7	媽ㄇㄚ媽˙ㄇㄚ	妈妈	māma	(N)mother
8	兩ㄌㄧㄤˇ	两	liǎng	(number)two

	Traditional Characters	Simplified Characters	Pinyin	English
9	妹ㄇㄟˋ妹˙ㄇㄟ	妹妹	mèimei	(N)younger sister
10	都ㄉㄡ	都	dōu	(Adv)all
11	可ㄎㄜˇ愛ㄞˋ	可爱	kěài	(Adj)cute

GRAMMAR

1. Someone + 有 + N
Someone + yǒu + N

Example:

Lin 有弟弟。

Lin 有弟弟。

Lin yǒu dìdi。

Lin has a younger brother.

2. NU + MW + N

Examples:

五個人

五个人

wǔ ge rén

five people

幾個人

几个人

jǐ ge rén

how many people

3. 這 + NU + MW

Zhè + NU + MW

Examples:

這兩個人

这两个人

zhè liǎng ge rén

these two people

LESSON 2

STORY

The bell rang at 12:05. Mark and Lin headed to the cafeteria for lunch to join Jeff, Jennifer and some other Kungfu Club members who were already eating there. Jennifer and Lin talk about their family members.

DIALOGUE

Jennifer：Lin，你的父母是哪裡人（Note）？
Lin，你的父母是哪里人（Note）？
Lin，nǐ de fùmǔ shì nǎlǐ rén ？

Lin：我父母都是臺灣人。
我父母都是台湾人。
Wǒ fùmǔ dōu shì Táiwān rén。

Mark：你們在家說中文嗎？
你们在家说中文吗？
Nǐmen zài jiā shuō Zhōngwén ma ？

Lin：對。Jennifer，你的父母是哪裡人？
对。Jennifer，你的父母是哪里人？
Duì。Jennifer，nǐ de fùmǔ shì nǎlǐ rén ？

Jennifer：我媽媽是上海人，爸爸是美國人。

我妈妈是上海人，爸爸是美国人。

Wǒ māma shì Shànghǎi rén，bàba shì Měiguó rén。

Note

對話2的句型，當中文說「○○○是哪裡人？」的意思就是英文的「○○○從哪來？」

In this dialogue there's an inconsistency with how the questions are asked and translations. 哪裡人doesn't really have an English equivalent. Translating this as "Where do your parents come from?" I think is a little misleading and confusing.

Jennifer: Lin, where are your parents from?
Lin: Both of my parents come from Taiwan.
Mark: Do you speak Mandarin at home?
Lin: Yes. Jennifer, where are your parents from?
Jennifer: My mother is from Shanghai. My father is American.

DISCUSSION

1. Where are Lin's parents from?
2. Where is Jennifer's mother from?
3. Does Lin speak Mandarin at home?

VOCABULARY

	Traditional Characters	Simplified Characters	Pinyin	English
1	父ㄈㄨˋ母ㄇㄨˇ 父ㄈㄨˋ、母ㄇㄨˇ	父母 父、母	fùmǔ fù、mǔ	(N) parents father, mother
2	哪ㄋㄚˇ裡ㄌㄧˇ	哪里	nǎlǐ	(Pro) where
3	在ㄗㄞˋ	在	zài	to be somewhere

TERM

	Traditional Characters	Simplified Characters	Pinyin	English
1	臺ㄊㄞˊ灣ㄨㄢ	台湾	Táiwān	Taiwan
2	上ㄕㄤˋ海ㄏㄞˇ	上海	Shànghǎi	Shanghai
3	美ㄇㄟˇ國ㄍㄨㄛˊ	美国	Měiguó	USA

EXPRESSION

	Traditional Characters	Simplified Characters	Pinyin	English
1	對ㄉㄨㄟˋ	对	duì	yes

GRAMMAR

1. N + 是 + 哪裡人？
N + shì + 哪裡人？
Where are you from?

Example:

你是哪裡人？
你是哪里人？
Nǐ shì nǎlǐ rén ？
Where are you from?

William 是哪裡人？
William 是哪里人？
William shì nǎlǐ rén ？
Where is William from?

2. Someone + 在 + pw

Example:

他在家。
他在家。
Tā zài jiā。
He is at home.

I. PRACTICE

1. 有 + 幾個 / 多少 + 人？

yǒu + jǐge/duōshǎo + rén

Q：你家有幾個人？

你家有几个人？

Nǐ jiā yǒu jǐge rén ？

How many people are there in your family?

A：我家有四個人。

我家有四个人。

Wǒ jiā yǒu sì ge rén。

There are four people in my family.

Practice

Q：你家有多少人？

你家有多少人？

Nǐ jiā yǒu duōshǎo rén ？

How many people are there in your family?

A：__________。

2. N + 是哪裡人？

N + shì nǎlǐ rén ？

Q：她是哪裡人？

她是哪里人？

Tā shì nǎlǐ rén ？

Where is she from?

A：她是上海人。

她是上海人。

Tā shì Shànghǎi rén。

She is from Shanghai.

Practice

Q：你是哪裡人？

你是哪里人？

Nǐ shì nǎlǐ rén？

Where are you from?

A：＿＿＿＿＿＿＿＿。

3. 在 + pw

zài + pw

Q：你在哪裡？

你在哪里？

Nǐ zài nǎlǐ？

Where are you?

A：我在家。

我在家。

Wǒ zài jiā。

I am home.

Practice

Q：Jeff 在哪裡？

Jeff 在哪里？

Jeff zài nǎlǐ？

Where is Jeff?

A：＿＿＿＿＿＿＿＿。

II. EXERCISE

1. Complete the following dialogue:

A：＿＿＿＿＿＿？

B：我家有四個人。

我家有四个人。

Wǒ jiā yǒu sì ge rén。

A：__________？

B：我是臺灣人。

我是台湾人。

Wǒ shì Táiwān rén。

A：你是哪裡人？

你是哪里人？

Nǐ shì nǎlǐ rén ？

B：__________。

2. Tasks

(1) Ask your classmates how many brothers and sisters they have.

(2) What is the average number of kids in your classmates' families?

III. SUPPLEMENTARY EXPLANATION

1. Numeral 零 - 十

Numeral	0	1	2	3	4	5	6
character	零	一	二	三	四	五	六
Pinyin	líng	yī	èr	sān	sì	wǔ	liù
Numeral	7	8	9	10	100	1000	10000
character	七	八	九	十	百	千	萬
Pinyin	qī	bā	jiǔ	shí	baǐ	qiān	wàn

2. Relative in Chinese

Relative	爺爺／祖父 爷爷／祖父	奶奶／祖母 奶奶／祖母	伯伯／叔叔 伯伯／叔叔	姑姑 姑姑	哥哥／弟弟 哥哥／弟弟	堂弟 堂弟
Pinyin	yéye/zŭfù	năinai/zŭmŭ	bóbo/shúshu	gūgū	gēge/dìdi	táng dì
English (from Father)	grandpa	grandma	uncle (elder/younger)	aunt	brother (elder/younger)	cousin
Relative	外公／外祖父 外公／外祖父	外婆／外祖母 外婆／外祖母	舅舅 舅舅	阿姨 阿姨	姊姊／姐姐 姊姊／姐姐	表姊／姐 表姊／姐
Pinyin	wàigōng/wàizŭfù	wàipó/wàizŭmŭ	jiùjiu	āyí	jiějie/jiějie	biăojiě/jiě
English (from Mother)	grandpa	grandma	uncle	aunt	elder sister	cousin

3. When one asks "幾個人几个人 jĭge rén" usually one does not anticipate the answer to be a large number of people. Therefore, this question is not suitable for asking the total population of a country.

Example:

What is the population of America?

美國有多少人？

美国有多少人？

Mĕiguó yŏu duōshăo rén ？

4. In Chinese, when one asks about the number of family members, another common measure word is "口 kŏu" because the number of family members indicates the number of mouths to feed.

Example:

How many mouths (persons) are there in your family?

5. You can omit the " 的 de" (possessive particle) between you and your family member or when you say "your family".

Example:

我姊姊

我姊姊

wǒ jiějie

my older sister

我爸爸

我爸爸

wǒ bàba

my father

我家

我家

wǒ jia

my family

6. The number "2," when used as a number, is pronounced as er4, and is written as the character 二 èr。 If it is followed by a measure word, then its pronunciation is liang3, and is written as the character 兩 两 liǎng。

Example:

兩個

两个

liǎng ge

兩桶
两桶（L6）
liǎng tǒng

兩家
两家（L7）
liǎng jiā

IV. CULTURAL NOTES

1. Three Generations Living Under One Roof（華人社會中的三代同堂）

A typical traditional Chinese family structure is referred to as "three generations living under one roof" meaning three generations (grandparents, parents, and children) living together in one household. Chinese people attach great importance to filial piety--being dutiful sons and daughters. The eldest son is obligated to take care of his parents for life and will live with them even after marriage along with his wife and kids. Husbands are expected to work while the wives serve their in-laws at home. Parents-in-laws will teach the young wife to be a homemaker and a good mother.

"Three generations living under one roof" has been practiced for thousands of years; however, social attitudes towards this family structure have gradually changed overtime. The traditional family pattern of "men outside the home, women inside the home" has changed due to the rise of feminist ideologies, leading to the emergence of "double-income families." Young couples are less willing to live with family elders and prefer to just live with their spouse and children. To strike a balance between being filial and attaining personal privacy, many families instead choose to be neighbors with three generations living in the same neighborhood.

2. Chinese Immigration in the U.S.（美國社會的華人移民轉變）

Chinese immigration to the U.S. started happening in large numbers in the 19th century--long before Jeremy Lin's family came to American from Taiwan in the 1970's.

In the 19th century over 300,000 Chinese immigrants flocked to California. Some in search of their fortune in the 1849-era Gold Rush, but many more for the safety of their families while hard times hit southern China. Many Chinese immigrants worked as laborers helping to create the First Transcontinental Railroad and foster California's agricultural system. Many immigrants faced much discrimination, and most were forced to relocate to Chinatowns.

Today in the United States, there are more than 3.3 million Chinese--about 1% of the total population, with ethnic Chinese people moving from China, Taiwan and Southeast Asia and in ever growing numbers.

第四章
UNIT 4

Please come over to my house.
請你來我家

Warm Up Activities

1. What is your favorite day of the week? Why?
2. Do you like parties? What do you usually do at parties?

LESSON 1

STORY

This afternoon, the basketball team is practicing for a tournament next month. During the break, Lin invites Mark to his house for a Mid-Autumn Festival party this Saturday. Lin's relatives in Taiwan always have barbecue and moon cake on this festival. Lin's mother asked Lin to invite some friends to join their party.

DIALOGUE

Lin：Mark，你這周末有空嗎？
Mark，你这周末有空吗？
Mark，nǐ zhè zhōumò yǒukòng ma ？

Mark：星期六嗎？有！
星期六吗？有！
Xīngqí liù ma ？ Yǒu ！

Lin：那天是中秋節，我想請你們來我家烤肉。
那天是中秋节，我想请你们来我家烤肉。
Nàtiān shì Zhōngqiūjié，wǒ xiǎng qǐng nǐmen lái wǒjiā kǎoròu。

Mark：太好了，沒問題，我可以去！
太好了，没问题，我可以去！
Tàihǎole，méiwèntí，wǒ kěyǐ qù ！

Lin: Mark, do you have free time on Saturday?
Mark: Saturday? Yes!
Lin: It's Mid-Autumn Festival. I want to invite you to my house for barbecue.
Mark: That's wonderful. No problem. I can go!

DISCUSSION

1. Does Mark have free time on Saturday?
2. What is Lin going to do on Saturday?
3. Why is Lin inviting Mark to his house?

VOCABULARY

	Traditional Characters	Simplified Characters	Pinyin	English
1	周ㄓㄡ末ㄇㄛˋ	周末	zhōumò	(N) weekend
2	有ㄧㄡˇ空ㄎㄨㄥˋ	有空	yǒukòng	(V) to have free time
3	星ㄒㄧㄥ期ㄑㄧˊ 星ㄒㄧㄥ期ㄑㄧˊ六ㄌㄧㄡˋ 星ㄒㄧㄥ期ㄑㄧˊ天ㄊㄧㄢ	星期 星期六 星期天	xīngqí xīngqí liù xīngqí tiān	(N) week (N) Saturday (N) Sunday
4	那ㄋㄚˋ	那	nà	(Pro) that
5	天ㄊㄧㄢ	天	tiān	(N) day
6	想ㄒㄧㄤˇ	想	xiǎng	(V) to want
7	請ㄑㄧㄥˇ	请	qǐng	(V) to invite
8	太ㄊㄞˋ	太	tài	(Adv) too
9	可ㄎㄜˇ以ㄧˇ	可以	kěyǐ	(AV) can, may
10	來ㄌㄞˊ	来	lái	(V) to come
11	去ㄑㄩˋ	去	qù	(V) to go

TERM

	Traditional Characters	Simplified Characters	Pinyin	English
1	中ㄓㄨㄥ秋ㄑㄧㄡ節ㄐㄧㄝˊ	中秋节	Zhōngqiūjié	Mid-Autumn Festival
2	烤ㄎㄠˇ肉ㄖㄡˋ	烤肉	kǎoròu	barbecue

EXPRESSION

	Traditional Characters	Simplified Characters	Pinyin	English
1	太好了	太好了	tàihǎole	wonderful
2	沒問題	没问题	méiwèntí	no problem
3	問題	问题	wèntí	problem

GRAMMAR

1. Someone + a specific time + V

Example:

你星期六有空嗎？

你星期六有空吗？

Nǐ xīngqí liù yǒukòng ma ？

Do you have time on Saturday?

2. Someone + 請 + someone + V
Someone + qǐng + someone + V

Example:

我請你來我家。

我请你来我家。

Wǒ qǐng nǐ lái wǒ jiā。

I invite you to come to my house.

LESSON 2

STORY

The basketball team had just finished their practice. On the way home, Lin and Mark ran into Linda and Maria who were heading to the gym for their cheerleading practice. Lin also invited Linda and Maria to his barbecue party. Knowing that Mark would be there, Lin and Maria also promised to go. Lin needs Linda and Maria's cell phone number for further communication.

DIALOGUE

Lin：我們明天烤肉，你們可以來嗎？
我们明天烤肉，你们可以来吗？
Wǒmen míngtiān kǎoròu，nǐmen kěyǐ lái ma ？

Linda：烤肉很有意思！ Maria，妳去嗎？
烤肉很有意思！ Maria，你去吗？
Kǎoròu hěnyǒuyìsi ！ Maria，nǐ qù ma ？

Maria：行啊，我喜歡烤肉！
行啊，我喜欢烤肉。
Xíng a，wǒ xǐhuān kǎoròu ！

Lin：妳的手機是幾號？
你的手机是几号？
Nǐ de shǒujī shì jǐhào ？

Linda：807-5126。(to Maria) 我們一起去吧！
807-5126。(to Maria) 我们一起去吧！
Bā líng qī - wǔ yī èr liù。(to Maria) Wǒmen yìqǐ qù ba ！

Lin: We'll have a barbecue tomorrow. Can you come?
Linda: Barbeque is interesting. Maria, do you want to go?
Maria: Yes, I like barbecue!
Lin: What is your cell phone number?
Linda: 807-5126. (Turns to Maria) Let's go together.

DISCUSSION

1. Who did Lin invite to his barbeque party?
2. What is Linda's cell phone number?

VOCABULARY

	Traditional Characters	Simplified Characters	Pinyin	English
1	明ㄇㄧㄥˊ天ㄊㄧㄢ	明天	míngtiān	(N) tomorrow
2	啊˙ㄚ	啊	a	a phrase final particle, indicates affirmation
3	手ㄕㄡˇ機ㄐㄧ	手机	shǒujī	(N) cellphone
4	號ㄏㄠˋ	号	hào	(N) number
5	一ㄧˋ起ㄑㄧˇ	一起	yìqǐ	(Adv) together

EXPRESSION

	Traditional Characters	Simplified Characters	Pinyin	English
1	很有意思	很有意思	hěnyǒuyìsi	that's very interesting
2	行啊	行啊	xíng a	yes (stress affirmative)

GRAMMAR

1. Someone + 可以 + V + 嗎 (ma) ？

Someone + kěyǐ + V + 吗 (ma) ？

Example:

你可以來嗎？

你可以来吗？

Nǐ kěyǐ lái ma ？

Can you come?

2. 一起 + V

yìqǐ + V

Example:

我們一起去。

我们一起去。

Wǒmen yìqǐ qù。

Let's go together.

I. PRACTICE

1. 星期（xīngqí）

Q：明天星期幾？
明天星期几？
Míngtiān xīngqí jǐ ？
What day is tomorrow?

A：明天星期三。
明天星期三。
Míngtiān xīngqí sān。
Tomorrow is Wednesday.

Practice

Q：今天星期幾？
今天星期几？
Jīntiān xīngqí jǐ ？
What day is today?

A：＿＿＿＿＿＿＿＿。

2. TW + 有空
TW + yǒukòng

Q：妳明天有空嗎？
你明天有空吗？
Nǐ míngtiān yǒukòng ma ？
Do you have free time tomorrow?

A：我明天有空。
我明天有空。
Wǒ míngtiān yǒukòng。
I have free time tomorrow.

Practice

Q：你星期六有空嗎？

你星期六有空吗？

Nǐ xīngqí liù yǒukòng ma ？

Do you have free time on Saturday?

A：________________。

3. 我想請你 + V

Wǒ xiǎng qǐng nǐ + V

Q：我想請你來我家打籃球。

我想请你来我家打篮球。

Wǒ xiǎng qǐng nǐ lái wǒjiā dǎ lánqiú。

I want to invite you to my house to play basketball.

A：好啊。

好啊。

Hǎo a。

Alright.

Q：我想請你……

我想请你……

Wǒ xiǎng qǐng nǐ……

I want to invite you to ...

A：________________。

II. EXERCISE

1. Complete the following dialogue:

A：____________？

B：今天星期五。
今天星期五。
Jīn tiān xīngqí wǔ。

A：__________？

B：這個周末我沒空。
这个周末我没空。
Zhège zhōumò wǒ méikòng。

A：我想請你來我家烤肉。
我想请你来我家烤肉。
Wǒ xiǎng qǐng nǐ lái wǒjiā kǎoròu。

B：__________。

2. Tasks

Invite your classmate to come to your house this weekend.

How many of them can come to your house?

III. SUPPLEMENTARY EXPLANATION

1. 星期的說法

Week	星期天（日） 星期天（日）	星期一 星期一	星期二 星期二	星期三 星期三	星期四 星期四	星期五 星期五	星期六 星期六
Pinyin	xīngqí tiān (rì)	xīngqí yī	xīngqí èr	xīngqí sān	xīngqí sì	xīngqí wǔ	xīngqí liù
English	Sunday	Monday	Tuesday	Wednesday	Thursday	Friday	Saturday

2. When talking about days of the week or days, sometimes you can omit the "to be" verb " 是 shì." For example:

明天（是）星期五。

明天（是）星期五。

Míngtiān (shì) xīngqí wǔ。

Tomorrow will be Friday.

However, this rule does not apply when you are talking about holidays. For example:

那一天是中秋節。

那一天是中秋节。

Nàyìtiān shì Zhōngqiūjié。

That day is Mid-Autumn festival.

3. For days of the week, you can either say 星期 xīngqí or 禮拜 礼拜 lǐbài.

星期一＝禮拜一

Xīngqí yī = Lǐbài yī

4. Sunday can either be 星期天 Xīngqí tiān or 星期日 Xīngqí rì.

5. When placed at the end of the sentence responding to a request or invitation, "啊 a" serves two purposes. It stresses the willingness of the respondent to accept the invitation, and also softens the tone of voice so it does not sound too abrupt or hasty.

6. Mid-Autumn Festival 中秋節 Zhōngqiūjié is one of the most important Chinese festivals. It is on August 15th of the Lunar Calendar.

IV. CULTURAL NOTES

1. Origin of the Mid-Autumn Festival（華人的中秋節及由來）

Mid-Autumn Festival (Moon Festival) is on August 15th of the lunar calendar, exactly a full moon right in the middle of autumn. The most famous legend about this holiday is the story of a Chinese beauty flying to the Moon. The legend starts with there being nine blazing suns in the ancient sky making survival difficult for mankind. A hero named Hou Yi shot down eight of the suns to save the common people, and as a result, earned his position as their ruler. The Heavenly Queen Mother rewarded him the elixir of life. Hou Yi gradually became tyrannical so his wife, Chang-er, who could not bear see people suffer from her husband's rule, decided to steal his immortality elixir and then flew to the moon. The common people expressed their gratitude for Chang-er's sacrifice by making August 15th on the lunar calendar a day to worship and pray for peace and prosperity to Chang-er. This day later became a holiday for family reunions, where families would gather to gaze at the full moon while eating moon cakes and grape fruits.

Taiwan celebrated Mid-Autumn Festival the traditional way up until 1987 when a successful soy sauce ad started promoting barbequing on this holiday. Therefore, in the past 20 years, it is customary for family and friends to gather on the side of the streets under the full moon with small grills barbequing while eating moon cakes and grapefruits.

2.Food on Chinese Holidays（中國特別的節慶食物）

The Chinese attach great importance to food and important holidays will be celebrated by eating certain foods, as there are rich cultural meanings behind them. Let's get familiar with the foods of some major traditional Chinese festivals: the Spring Festival, the Lantern festival, the Dragon Boat Festival, and the Mid-Autumn Festival.

The Spring Festival, also called Chinese New Year, begins either in January or February depending on the lunar calendar. Cooking or purchasing rice cakes is popular during this holiday because "rice cakes" sounds like "escalating yearly" in Chinese, which brings hope that the new year will be a better year. People will also eat dumplings because the shape of dumplings resembles traditional Chinese money, which represents fortune. They believe that eating these foods will bring good luck.

Lantern festival is a holiday on January 15th of the lunar calendar, the last day of the New Year period. On that day, people like to eat sweet ball-shaped dumplings that represent harmony in the family.

For the Dragon Boat Festival, people eat glutinous rice with other ingredients wrapped in bamboo leaves to commemorate Qu Yuan, an ancient poet in 280 BC. On Mid-Autumn Festival, traditionally, people eat moon cakes and grapefruits, but in recent years, Taiwan celebrates this holiday by barbequing with friends and family.

You can see these foods in Chinese supermarkets in the US at certain times in the year.

第五章

UNIT 5

What day is your birthday?

你的生日是什麼時候？

Warm Up Activities

1. What is your favorite number? Why?
2. How do you celebrate your birthday? Do you celebrate your birthday the same way you did when you were younger?

LESSON 1

STORY

At Lin's Mid-Autumn Festival barbecue party, Mark arrived early to shoot some hoops. Lin also invited Jeff and Jennifer from the Kungfu Club. Mark is happy to see them and goes into the living room to say hello to them. Maria and Linda were singing karaoke when Jeff and Jennifer arrived. Lin tries to introduce them to each other.

DIALOGUE

Mark：Jennifer，你們也來了！
Jennifer，你们也来了！
Jennifer，nǐmen yě lái le ！

Jeff：Lin，今天是你的生日嗎？
Lin，今天是你的生日吗？
Lin，jīntiān shì nǐ de shēngrì ma ？

Lin：不是，今天是中國的中秋節。
不是，今天是中国的中秋节。
Bú shì，jīntiān shì Zhōngguó de Zhōngqiūjié。

Linda：Lin，你的生日是什麼時候？
Lin，你的生日是什么时候？

Lin，nǐ de shēngrì shì shénme shíhòu ？

Lin：是九月二十八日。
是九月二十八日。
Shì Jiǔ yuè èrshíbā rì。

Mark: Jennifer, you're here!
Jeff: Lin, is today your birthday?
Lin: No. Today is the Chinese Mid-Autumn festival.
Linda: Lin, when is your birthday?
Lin: It is on September 28th.

DISCUSSION

1. Is today Lin's birthday?
2. What day is Lin's birthday?

VOCABULARY

	Traditional Characters	Simplified Characters	Pinyin	English
1	了˙ㄌㄜ	了	le	(P) particle indicating the completion of the action.
2	生ㄕㄥ 日ㄖˋ	生日	shēngrì	(N) birthday
3	時ㄕˊ 候ㄏㄡˋ	时候	shíhòu	(N) time
4	月ㄩㄝˋ	月	yuè	(N) month
5	日ㄖˋ	日	rì	(N) day

GRAMMAR

1. ……是什麼時候？

……**shì shénme shíhòu**？

Example:

你的生日是什麼時候？

你的生日是什么时候？

Nǐ de shēngrì shì shénme shíhòu？

When is your birthday?

2. Certain holiday or special day + 是……月……日
Certain holiday or special day + shì... yuè... rì

Example:

中秋節是八月十五日。

中秋节是八月十五日。

Zhōngqiūjié shì Bā yuè shíwǔ rì。

Mid-Autumn Festival is on August 15th.

LESSON 2

STORY

The moon is big, round and bright. Lin and his classmates are chatting while they are enjoying the barbecue meal. At the same time, they are also sipping on Chinese tea and eating moon cakes (a special dessert for Mid-Autumn Festival.)

DIALOGUE

Linda：Lin，下星期五是你的生日！我們一起吃飯吧！
Lin，下星期五是你的生日！我们一起吃饭吧！
Lin，xià xīngqí wǔ shì nǐ de shēngrì ！ Wǒmen yìqǐ chī fàn ba ！

Maria：眞的！我可以做一個蛋糕。
真的！我可以做一个蛋糕。
Zhēnde ！ Wǒ kěyǐ zuò yí ge dàngāo。

Jennifer：Lin，你今年幾歲？
Lin，你今年几岁？
Lin，nǐ jīnnián jǐ suì ？

Lin：我十七歲，Jeff，你呢？
　　我十七岁，Jeff，你呢？
　　Wǒ shíqī suì，Jeff，nǐ ne ？

Jeff：我十六歲。
　　我十六岁。
　　Wǒ shíliù suì。

> Linda: Lin, next Friday is your birthday! Let's all have dinner together.
> Maria: Really! I can make a cake.
> Jennifer: Lin, how old are you this year?
> Lin: I am seventeen. How about you, Jeff?
> Jeff: I am sixteen.

DISCUSSION

1. What will Maria make for Lin's birthday?
2. How old is Jeff?

VOCABULARY

	Traditional Characters	Simplified Characters	Pinyin	English
1	下星期	下星期	xià xīngqí	(N) next week
2	吃飯	吃饭	chī fàn	(V) have a meal
3	吧	吧	ba	question particle indicating a request
4	做	做	zuò	(V) to make
5	蛋糕	蛋糕	dàngāo	(N) cake

	Traditional Characters	Simplified Characters	Pinyin	English
6	今ㄐㄧㄣ年ㄋㄧㄢˊ	今年	jīnnián	(TW) this year
7	歲ㄙㄨㄟˋ	岁	suì	measure word for age

EXPRESSION

	Traditional Characters	Simplified Characters	Pinyin	English
1	真ㄓㄣ的ㄉㄜ˙	真的	zhēnde	really
2	你ㄋㄧˇ呢ㄋㄜ˙？	你呢?	nǐ ne	how about you?

GRAMMAR

…，S. + 呢？

…，S. + ne ？

Example:

我不會說中文，你呢？

我不会说中文，你呢？

Wǒ búhuì shuō Zhōngwén，nǐ ne ？

I can not speak Mandarin. How about you?

我很喜歡烤肉，你呢？

我很喜欢烤肉，你呢？

Wǒ hěn xǐhuān kǎoròu，nǐ ne ？

I like barbecue very much. How about you?

I. PRACTICE

1.

Q：中秋節是什麼時候？
中秋节是什么时候？
Zhōngqiūjié shì shénme shíhòu ？
When is the Mid-Autumn Festival?

A：中秋節是八月十五日。
中秋节是八月十五日。
Zhōngqiūjié shì Bā yuè shíwǔ rì。
Mid-Autumn Festival is on August 15th of the Lunar calendar.

Practice

Q：你的生日是什麼時候？
你的生日是什么时候？
Nǐ de shēngrì shì shénme shíhòu ？
When is your birthday?

A：________________。

2.

Q：你的生日是幾月幾號？
你的生日是几月几号？
Nǐ de shēngrì shì jǐ yuè jǐ hào ？
When is your birthday?

A：我的生日是九月十號。
我的生日是九月十号。
Wǒ de shēngrì shì jiǔ yuè shí hào。
My birthday is on September 10th.

Practice

Q：中國新年是幾月幾號？

中国新年是几月几号？

Zhōngguóxīnnián shì jǐ yuè jǐ hào ？

When is Chinese New Year?

A：________________。

3.

Q：我喜歡中文，你呢？

我喜欢中文，你呢？

Wǒ hěn xǐhuān Zhōngwén，nǐ ne ？

I like Mandarin. How about you?

A：我也喜歡。

我也喜欢。

Wǒ yě xǐhuān。

I also like Mandarin.

Practice

Q：我明天有空，你呢？

我明天有空，你呢？

Wǒ míngtiān yǒukòng，nǐ ne ？

I have some free time tomorrow. How about you?

A：________________。

II. EXERCISE

Complete the following dialogue:

A：__________？

B：今天星期五。

今天星期五。

Jīntiān xīngqí wǔ。

A：__________？

B：明天八月五號。

明天八月五号。

Míngtiān bā yuè wǔ hào。

A：__________？

B：這個周末我沒空。

这个周末我没空。

Zhège zhōumò wǒ méikòng。

III. SUPPLEMENTARY EXPLANATION

1. 月份說法

Month	一月	二月	三月	四月	五月	六月
Pinyin	Yì yuè	Èr yuè	Sān yuè	Sì yuè	Wǔ yuè	Liù yuè
English	January	February	March	April	May	June
Numeral	七月	八月	九月	十月	十一月	十二月
Pinyin	Qī yuè	Bā yuè	Jiǔ yuè	Shí yuè	Shíyī yuè	Shíèr yuè
English	July	August	September	October	November	December

2. 吧 ba is a sentence suffix to soften the tone of voice so that it sounds more polite.
3. 呢 ne can be used to form a tag question which allows one to ask a question without using the question word.

Examples:

我是美國人，你（是哪國人）呢？

我是美国人，你（是哪国人）呢？

Wǒ shì Měiguó rén，nǐ (shì năguó rén) ne ？

I am American. Which country are you from?

→ 我是美國人，你呢？

我是美国人，你呢？

Wǒ shì Měiguó rén，nǐ ne ？

I am American, how about you?

我喜歡中文，你（喜歡什麼）呢？

我喜欢中文，你（喜欢什么）呢？

Wǒ xǐhuān Zhōngwén，nǐ (xǐhuān shénme) ne ？

I like Mandarin. What do you like?

→ 我喜歡中文，你呢？

我喜欢中文，你呢？

Wǒ xǐhuān Zhōngwén，nǐ ne ？

I like Mandarin. How about you?

IV. CULTURAL NOTES

1. Celebrating Birthdays in China（中國人的慶生方式）

No American birthday party would be complete without some kind of cake filled with candles at the end, right? So what is it like to celebrate one's birthday in China or Taiwan? Nowadays, birthday cakes are just as common in Asia as they are in the states, and they are generally accompanied by a quick round of "Happy Birthday" in English by all those gathered to celebrate. However, rather than everyone choosing just how big a slice of cake they want, it's up to the host to split the cake as evenly as possible for everyone. A more traditional style birthday party might also include a small bowl of 長壽麵 (longevity noodles), which brings good luck, and of course, long life to whomever eats the dish.

While it is expected to give gifts at a birthday party, don't be alarmed if your friend doesn't open any of their gifts in front of you. It is considered rather rude to open a gift in front of others, especially in the rare scenario that they get something they really dislike! So next time you celebrate a birthday with your Chinese friends, don't be scared, it will be more similar than you think. Just be ready to eat your share of the cake, no matter how big the piece!

2.Chinese Zodiac（中國的生肖）

Instead of asking for someone's age directly, many Chinese people would ask, "What's your Chinese zodiac animal?" 你屬什麼？ Nǐ shǔ shénme ？ In asking so, one's age can be calculated. For example, if you were born in 1996 and say that your Chinese zodiac animal is the Rat, the person asking will guess that you are sixteen-years-old.

The Chinese zodiac is widely used in East Asian countries such as Vietnam, Korea, and Japan. It is similar to the Western zodiac where there's a time cycle divided into twelve parts. However, the Chinese zodiac cycle corresponds to years rather than months, with each year being represented by an animal. The twelve animals in sequential order are: Rat, ox, tiger, rabbit, dragon, snake, horse, goat, monkey, rooster, dog, and pig. Each animal carries attributes that serve as a predictor of your personality as well as your compatibility with others. For instance, if your zodiac animal is a Pig (born in 1995), your animal symbolizes character traits such as diligence, compassion, and generosity. Also, you are most compatible with a Rabbit and Goat.

第六章 UNIT 6

How do you get to the Chinese supermarket?

到中國超市怎麼走？

Warm Up Activities

1. Have you ever been lost? What did you do when you got lost?
2. When looking for a place you've never been to before, do you use a map or GPS?

LESSON 1

STORY

Halloween is approaching and the Chinese Kungfu Club members are busy preparing for their annual fundraising activity. Every year the Chinese Kungfu Club sells something to raise funds to buy books for an elementary school located in a remote area in China. Lin came up with the idea of selling pearl milk tea for this year's fundraising event. As it is fun and delicious, everyone agrees to give it a try. Lin's mother gave them the recipe and showed them how to make it. This morning, Jennifer, Jeff, and Mark went to a Chinese supermarket in Flushing, Queens to buy the ingredients but ended up getting lost. Jennifer decides to ask an old Chinese man selling newspapers for directions.

DIALOGUE

Jennifer：請問，附近有沒有中國超市？
请问，附近有没有中国超市?
Qǐngwèn，fùjìn yǒuméiyǒu Zhōngguó chāoshì ？

Clerk：有啊！在三十八街。
有啊！在三十八街。
Yǒu a ！ Zài sānshíbā jiē。

Jeff：請問，到那兒怎麼走？
请问，到那儿怎么走？
Qǐngwèn，dào nàer zěnme zǒu ？

Clerk：你往東走，過兩個路口左轉，超市在你的右邊。
你往东走，过两个路口左转，超市在你的右边。
Nǐ wǎng dōng zǒu，guò liǎng ge lùkǒu zuǒ zhuǎn，chāoshì zài nǐ de yòu biān。

Jeff：對不起，請再說一次！
对不起，请再说一次！
Duìbùqǐ，qǐng zài shuō yícì ！

Jennifer: Excuse me. Is there a Chinese supermarket around here?
Old man: Yes, on 38th street.
Jeff: Can you please tell us how to get there?
Old man: Go east and after you pass two intersections, turn left. The supermarket will be on your right side.
Jeff: Sorry, can you say that again?

DISCUSSION

1. Where are Jennifer, Jeff, and Mark going?
2. Does Jeff understand the directions to the supermarket?

VOCABULARY

	Traditional Characters	Simplified Characters	Pinyin	English
1	到ㄉㄠˋ	到	dào	(V) to go to
2	附ㄈㄨˋ近ㄐㄧㄣˋ	附近	fùjìn	(N) nearby
3	超ㄔㄠ 市ㄕˋ	超市	chāoshì	(N) supermarket
4	街ㄐㄧㄝ	街	jiē	(N) street
5	那ㄋㄚˋ兒ㄦ	那儿	nàer	(Adv) there
6	往ㄨㄤˇ	往	wǎng	to go toward
7	東ㄉㄨㄥ	东	dōng	(N, PW) east
8	走ㄗㄡˇ	走	zǒu	(V) to walk
9	過ㄍㄨㄛˋ	过	guò	(V) to pass
10	路ㄌㄨˋ口ㄎㄡˇ	路口	lùkǒu	(N) intersection
11	再ㄗㄞˋ	再	zài	(Adv) again

	Traditional Characters	Simplified Characters	Pinyin	English
12	左轉	左转	zuǒ zhuǎn	(V) to turn left
13	右邊	右边	yòu biān	(N) right side

EXPRESSION

	Traditional Characters	Simplified Characters	Pinyin	English
1	請問	请问	qǐngwèn	excuse me
2	對不起	对不起	duìbùqǐ	sorry
3	請再說一次	请再说一次	qǐng zài shuō yícì	please say that again
4	請	请	qǐng	please

GRAMMAR

1. 到 + some place + 怎麼走？
dào + some place + zěnme zǒu ？

Example:

到公車站怎麼走？

到公车站怎么走？

Dào gōngchēzhàn zěnme zǒu ？

How do you get to the bus stop?

2. N + 在哪兒？

N + zài nǎr ？

Example:

鞋子在哪兒？

鞋子在哪儿？

Xiézi zài nǎr ？

Where are the shoes?

3. N + 在 + some place

N +zài + some place

Example:

我在公車站。

我在公车站。

Wǒ zài gōngchēzhàn。

I am at the bus stop.

4. Someone + 往 + direction + 走

Someone + wǎng + direction + zǒu

Example:

你往東走。

你往东走。

Nǐ wǎng dōng zǒu。

Walk toward the east.

LESSON 2

STORY

The fundraising event is held at the community center. On Saturday morning, the Kungfu Club members are carrying everything to the gate of the community center. Maria and Jennifer are responsible for cooking the pearls, Jeff and Mark are to make the black tea and prepare the sugar, while Lin's job is to collect money. Linda made a flyer saying "The Captain's Pearl Milk Tea — Raise Funds for Elementary School Textbooks in a Remote Area of China." Their pearl milk tea is very popular. Mark wants to go to the bathroom, but does not know where it is. He asks Jeff if he knows where the bathroom is.

DIALOGUE

Mark：Jeff，你知道廁所在哪裡？我要去洗手。
Jeff，你知道厕所在哪里？我要去洗手。
Jeff，nǐ zhīdào cèsuǒ zài nǎlǐ ？ Wǒ yào qù xǐshǒu。

Jeff：男生廁所在二樓，上樓右轉。
男生厕所在二楼，上楼右转。
Nánshēng cèsuǒ zài èrlóu，shàng lóu yòu zhuǎn。

Jennifer：Jeff，奶茶不夠，怎麼辦？
Jeff，奶茶不够，怎么办？
Jeff，nǎichá bú gòu，zěnmebàn ？

Jeff：別擔心，桌子下面有兩桶。
别担心，桌子下面有两桶。
Biédānxīn，zhuōzi xià miàn yǒu liǎng tǒng。

Jennifer：可是桶子裡面沒有東西！
可是桶子里面没有东西！
Kěshì tǒngzi lǐ miàn méiyǒu dōngxi ！

> Mark: Jeff, do you know where the restroom is? I want to wash my hands.
> Jeff: The men's restroom is on the second floor. Go upstairs and turn right.
> Jennifer: Jeff, we are running out of milk tea. What are we going to do?
> Jeff: Don't worry. There are two tubs [of milk tea] under the table.
> Jennifer: But there is nothing in the barrels!

DISCUSSION

1. Where is the men's restroom?
2. Is there any milk tea left?

VOCABULARY

	Traditional Characters	Simplified Characters	Pinyin	English
1	知ㄓ道ㄉㄠˋ	知道	zhīdào	(V) know
2	廁ㄘㄜˋ所ㄙㄨㄛˇ	厕所	cèsuǒ	(N) bathroom

	Traditional Characters	Simplified Characters	Pinyin	English
3	要	要	yào	(AV) to want to
4	洗手	洗手	xǐshǒu	(V) to wash hands
5	男生	男生	nánshēng	(N) men
6	上樓	上楼	shàng lóu	(V) to go upstairs
7	奶茶	奶茶	nǎichá	(N) milk tea
8	夠	够	gòu	(Adj) enough
9	桌子	桌子	zhuōzi	(N) table
10	下面	下面	xià miàn	(N) under
11	桶	桶	tǒng	(MW) tub
12	桶子	桶子	tǒngzi	(N) barrel
13	裡面	里面	lǐ miàn	(N) inside
14	東西	东西	dōngxi	(N) things

EXPRESSION

	Traditional Characters	Simplified Characters	Pinyin	English
1	怎麼辦？	怎么办?	zěnmebàn	what are we going to do?
2	別擔心	别担心	biédānxīn	don't worry

GRAMMAR

1. Something + 在哪裡？

Something + zài nălǐ？

Example:

廁所在哪裡？

厕所在哪里？

Cèsuŏ zài nălǐ ？

Where is the bathroom?

2. N + 裡面 + 有 + N2

N + lǐ miàn + yǒu + N2

Example:

桶子裡面沒有奶茶。

桶子里面没有奶茶。

Tǒngzi lǐ miàn méiyǒu năichá。

There is nothing in the tub.

I. PRACTICE

1.

Q：到中國超商怎麼走？

到中国超商怎么走？

Dào Zhōngguó chāoshāng zěnme zǒu ？

How do you get to the Chinese supermarket?

A：你往東走，過兩個路口，就到了。

你往东走，过两个路口，就到了。

Nǐ wăng dōng zǒu，guò liăng ge lùkǒu，jiù dào le。

You can head east, cross two intersections, and you’re there.

Practice

Q：到你的學校怎麼走？

到你的学校怎么走？

Dào nǐ de xuéxiào zěnme zǒu ？

How to get to your school?

A：________________。

2.

Q：男生廁所在哪裡？

男生厕所在哪里？

Nánshēng cèsuǒ zài nǎlǐ ？

Where is the men's restroom?

A：在二樓，上樓右轉。

在二楼，上楼右转。

Zài èr lóu，shàng lóu yòu zhuǎn。

On the second floor. Go upstairs and turn right.

Practice

Q：女生廁所在哪裡？

女生厕所在哪里？

Nǚshēng cèsuǒ zài nǎlǐ ？

Where is lady's room?

A：________________。

3.

Q：桌子下面有什麼？

桌子下面有什么？

Zhuōzi xià miàn yǒu shénme ？

What is under the table?

A：桌子下面有兩桶奶茶。
桌子下面有两桶奶茶。
Zhuōzi xià miàn yǒu liǎng tǒng nǎichá。
There are two tubs of milk tea under the table.

Practice

Q：你的桌子上面有什麼？
你的桌子上面有什么？
Nǐ de zhuōzi shàng miàn yǒu shénme ？
What is on your table?
A：＿＿＿＿＿＿＿＿。

II. EXERCISE

1. Complete the following dialogue:

A：到公車站怎麼走？
到公车站怎么走？
Dào gōngchēzhàn zěnme zǒu ？
B：＿＿＿＿＿＿。

A：廁所在哪裡？
厕所在哪里？
Cèsuǒ zài nǎlǐ ？
B：廁所在＿＿＿＿＿＿。
Cèsuǒ zài＿＿＿＿＿＿。

A：＿＿＿＿＿＿？
B：書包裡面有兩本書。
背包里面有两本书。
Shūbāo lǐ miàn yǒu liǎng běn shū。

2. Task

Introduce a store near the school and give us directions to get there.

III. SUPPLEMENTARY NOTES

1. 哪裡 哪里 nǎlǐ and 哪兒 哪儿 nǎr are both question words to ask locations. In China, people use 哪兒 哪儿 nǎr more often and in Taiwan, people usually use 哪裡 哪里 nǎlǐ.

2. Positional Nouns 方位詞

Directions	上面 上面	下面 下面	裡面 里面	外面 外面	左邊 左边	右邊 右边
Pinyin	shàng miàn	xià miàn	lǐ miàn	wài miàn	zuǒ biān	yòu biān
English	upside	beneath	inside	outside	left	right
Position	東 东	西 西	南 南	北 北	東北／西北 东北／西北	東南／西南 东南／西南
Pinyin	dōng	xī	nán	běi	dōng běi/xī běi	dōng nán/xī nán
English	east	west	south	north	northeast/north-west	southeast/south-west

3. 廁所 厕所 cèsuǒ (bathroom)，can also be called 洗手間 洗手间 xǐshǒujiān (washing room) or 衛生間 卫生间 wèishēngjiān (cleaning room).

IV. CULTURAL NOTES

1. Origin of the Chinatown (美國唐人街的由來)

The Tang Dynasty was a strong and wealthy period in Chinese history. Chinese people would refer to themselves as " 唐人 ," or "the people of Tang". As a result, places outside of China inhabited by large populations of Chinese, or "the Tang", came to be known as " 唐人街 " (Tang Avenue) or Chinatown.

Traditional Chinatowns, with over a hundred years of history, exist in over ten cities throughout North America including west coast cities of Los Angeles, San Francisco, Portland, Seattle, Vancouver, and Victoria. In the east coast, there's Boston, New York, Philadelphia, Washington, and many more. As for other regions, there's Chicago, Montreal, and Honolulu. However, despite the large number of Chinatowns, the ones in Los Angeles, San Francrsco and NewYork are the most popular. It seems as if it's not necessary to travel to China to experience and enjoy the Chinese atmosphere. There are always lots of people in Chinatown, especially during Chinese New Year. Want to have a delightful Chinese experience without going aboard? Just visit your nearest Chinatown!

2.Differences in Western and Eastern Chinese Children（深植於美國的社會服務觀念——美國華裔與亞洲孩子的不同）

In 2012, America's most famous Taiwanese-American is Jeremy Lin 林書豪 (Lín, Shū-Háo), a former basketball player for New York Knicks. In February of 2012, news about him dominated the news in Taiwan. Fans in Taiwan praised him not only for his athletic skills and academic accomplishments, but also for his humble character. He has become a role model to many kids in Taiwan.

American children possess different characteristics compared to children growing up in China or Taiwan. Education in the U.S. puts much emphasis on doing community service, as it has become an essential area many universities look at when reviewing college applications. In Asia, however, community service is less stressed. The Chinese society focuses more on family harmony and interests; therefore, they are more indifferent towards social issues.

3.Tiger Mother（虎媽對美國社會的震盪）

Chinese education is famous for the strict discipline enforced on children. One famous example is the Chinese 'Tiger Mom' whose extreme disciplinary style earned her an appearance on Time Magazine. This famous Tiger Mom is a professor in the U.S. who raised her two daughters the traditional Chinese way. She would not allow her daughters to watch T.V., participate in extra-curricular activities or sleep over at friends' houses. She expected her daughters to practice piano two hours a day and demanded straight A's from them. This strict traditional Chinese style of raising her daughters resulted in excellent report cards, but reccived much attention from the general public, which ignited the questions, "Is the traditional Chinese way of teaching necessarily helpful for the kids? How about the more lenient style of American education? Is it just as effective?"

For thousands of years, the 'Tiger Mom' way of parenting has been evident in Chinese society. This style of parenting may seem harsh and unforgiving, but it conveys a mother's hope and investment for her two daughters to succeed in the future. Although there are significant differences in the Asian and Western style of parenting, both cultures are successful in cultivating outstanding talents. Perhaps there is no such thing as one correct way of educating your child, but it's apparent that different cultures are capable of achieving the same results; and the reason behind these results is surely worthy of our attention.

第七章

UNIT 7

Let's have some Chinese Food.

我們去吃中國菜吧！

Warm Up Activities

1. Have you ever tried Chinese food? Do you like Chinese food?
2. Do any holidays you celebrate have any special dishes? How do they taste?

LESSON 1

STORY

Ever since the Kung Fu club's fundraising performance and food drive at the community center, Mark, Jennifer, Jeff, Linda, Maria, and Lin have been hanging out and having lunch together very often. Today, Lin brought sweet and sour pork that his mom made for him for lunch, and it made everyone envious. Jeff suggests that they should go out for Chinese food together sometime. Maria suggests an affordable and clean restaurant in China Town.

DIALOGUE

Jeff：這週末我們去吃中國菜，怎麼樣？
这周末我们去吃中国菜，怎么样？
Zhè zhōumò wǒmen qù chī Zhōngguócài，zěnmeyàng ？

Jennifer：好啊！哪家中國餐廳好？
好啊！哪家中国餐厅好？
Hǎo a ！ Nǎ jiā Zhōngguó cāntīng hǎo ？

Maria：聽說有一家四川菜不錯，在唐人街上。
听说有一家四川菜不错，在唐人街上。
Tīngshuō yǒu yì jiā Sìchuāncài búcuò，zài Tángrénjiē shàng。

Lin：嗯，我去過，口味很道地，也不太貴。
嗯，我去过，口味很道地，也不太贵。
En，wǒ qùguò，kǒuwèi hěn dàodì，yě bú tài guì。

Jeff：好！星期六中午十二點一刻見！
好！星期六中午十二点一刻见！
Hǎo ！ Xīngqí liù zhōngwǔ shíèr diǎn yí kè jiàn ！

Jeff: Let's go get Chinese food for lunch this Saturday. What do you think?
Jennifer: Sure. Which restaurant?
Maria: I've heard of a Sichuan restaurant that is pretty good. It's in China Town.
Lin: Yeah! I've been there. The food is really authentic and it's not too expensive.
Jeff: O.K. We'll meet at 12:15 on Saturday.

DISCUSSION

1. Where is the Sichuan restaurant?
2. What does Lin think of this restaurant?

VOCABULARY

	Traditional Characters	Simplified Characters	Pinyin	English
1	中ㄓㄨㄥ午ㄨˇ	中午	zhōngwǔ	(N) noon
2	家ㄐㄧㄚ	家	jiā	(MW) measure word for restaurants or stores
3	餐ㄘㄢ廳ㄊㄧㄥ	餐厅	cāntīng	(N) restaurant
4	不ㄅㄨˊ錯ㄘㄨㄛˋ	不错	búcuò	(SV) not bad
5	聽ㄊㄧㄥ說ㄕㄨㄛ	听说	tīngshuō	(V) hear/understand that
6	口ㄎㄡˇ味ㄨㄟˋ	口味	kǒuwèi	(N) flavor
7	道ㄉㄠˋ地ㄉㄧˋ	道地	dàodì	(SV) authentic
8	貴ㄍㄨㄟˋ	贵	guì	(SV) expensive
9	點ㄉㄧㄢˇ	点	diǎn	(N) o'clock
10	刻ㄎㄜˋ	刻	kè	(N) a quarter

TERM

	Traditional Characters	Simplified Characters	Pinyin	English
1	四ㄙˋ川ㄔㄨㄢ菜ㄘㄞˋ	四川菜	Sìchuāncài	Sichuan cuisine
2	唐ㄊㄤˊ人ㄖㄣˊ街ㄐㄧㄝ	唐人街	Tángrénjiē	China Town

EXPRESSION

	Traditional Characters	Simplified Characters	Pinyin	English
1	怎麼樣？	怎么样?	zěnmeyàng	what do you think?
2	我去過	我去过	wǒ qùguò	i have been there
3	走吧	走吧	zǒu ba	let's go

GRAMMAR

1. 哪 + Measure word + N + SV ？
Nǎ + Measure word + N + SV ？

Example:

哪家餐廳好？

哪家餐厅好？

Nǎ jiā cāntīng hǎo ？

Which restaurant is good?

2. So I have heard that...

Example:

聽説那家餐廳不错。

听说那家餐厅不错。

Tīngshuō nà jiā cāntīng búcuò。

I have heard that that restaurant is not bad.

3. V + 過 + N
V + guò + N

Example:

我去過那家餐廳。

我去过那家餐厅。

Wǒ qù guò nà jiā cāntīng。

I have been to that restaurant.

LESSON 2

STORY

The weather is really good this weekend. The Kungfu Club members arrive at the restaurant, which has big red lanterns at the entrance. The waiters are running in and out serving tea, and food from the dining hall gives off the fragrance of pepper and Fagara. The Kungfu Club find themselves a table and sit down. They look at the menu, trying to decide what to order.

DIALOGUE

Maria：這是菜單，你們想吃什麼？
这是菜单，你们想吃什么？
Zhè shì càidān，nǐmen xiǎng chī shéme ？

Linda：我們第一次來，請你介紹幾道菜吧！
我们第一次来，请你介绍几道菜吧！
Wǒmen dì yī cì lái，qǐng nǐ jièshào jǐ dào cài ba ！

Jennifer：這裡有名的菜都很辣，像麻婆豆腐、宮保雞丁都很好吃。
这里有名的菜都很辣，像麻婆豆腐、宫保鸡丁都很好吃。
Zhèlǐ yǒumíng de cài dōu hěn là，xiàng Mápódòufǔ、Gōngbǎojīdīng dōu hěn hǎochī。

Mark：有沒有不辣的？我不吃辣！
有没有不辣的？我不吃辣！
Yǒuméiyǒu bú là de ？ Wǒ bù chī là ！

Lin：但是四川菜全是辣的。
但是四川菜全是辣的。
Dànshì Sìchuāncài quán shì là de。

Maria: Here's the menu. What do you guys want to eat?
Linda: This is our first time here. Do you have any recommendations?
Jennifer: All of the specialty dishes, such as Mapou Tofu and Kungpao Chicked, are very spicy.
Mark: Is there anything that isn't spicy? I don't like spicy food.
Lin: But Sichuan food is all spicy!

DISCUSSION

1. What are the restaurant's specialties?
2. Does this restaurant serve non-spicy food?

VOCABULARY

	Traditional Characters	Simplified Characters	Pinyin	English
1	菜ㄘㄞˋ單ㄉㄢ	菜单	càidān	(N) menu
2	介ㄐㄧㄝˋ紹ㄕㄠˋ	介绍	jièshào	(V) to introduce
3	道ㄉㄠˋ	道	dào	measure word for dishes
4	菜ㄘㄞˋ	菜	cài	(N) dish
5	有ㄧㄡˇ名ㄇㄧㄥˊ	有名	yǒumíng	(SV) famous
6	辣ㄌㄚˋ	辣	là	(SV) spicy
7	好ㄏㄠˇ吃ㄔ	好吃	hǎochī	(SV) delicious
8	但ㄉㄢˋ是ㄕˋ	但是	dànshì	(A) but
9	全ㄑㄩㄢˊ	全	quán	(A) all

TERM

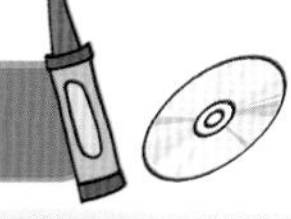

	Traditional Characters	Simplified Characters	Pinyin	English
1	麻ㄇㄚˊ婆ㄆㄛˊ豆ㄉㄡˋ腐ㄈㄨˇ	麻婆豆腐	Mápódòufǔ	Mapuo Tofu
2	宮ㄍㄨㄥ保ㄅㄠˇ雞ㄐㄧ丁ㄉㄧㄥ	宫保鸡丁	Gōngbǎojīdīng	Kungpao Chicken

EXPRESSION

	Traditional Characters	Simplified Characters	Pinyin	English
1	第ㄉㄧˋ一ㄧ次ㄘˋ	第一次	dì yī cì	the first time

GRAMMAR

1. ……，像 (such as) ……
……，xiàng (such as)……

Example:

這裡的菜都辣，像麻婆豆腐、宮保雞丁。

这里的菜都辣，像麻婆豆腐、宫保鸡丁。

Zhèlǐ de cài dōu là，xiàng Mápódòufǔ、Gōngbǎojīdīng。

The food here is all spicy, such as Mapuo Tofu and Kungpao Chicken.

2. maybe + S + can + Verb (give a suggestion)

Example:

你可以吃宮保雞丁。

你可以吃宫保鸡丁。

Nǐ kěyǐ chī Gōngbǎojīdīng。

Maybe you can have the Kungpao Chicken.

你可以說英文。

你可以说英文。

Nǐ kěyǐ shuō Yīngwén。

Maybe you can speak English.

I. PRACTICE

1.

Q：哪家中國餐廳好？

哪家中国餐厅好？

Nǎ jiā Zhōngguó cāntīng hǎo ？

Which Chinese restaurant is good?

A：聽說那家四川餐廳不錯。

听说那家四川餐厅不错。

Tīngshuō nà jiā Sìchuān cāntīng búcuò。

I have heard that Sichuan restaurant is not bad.

Practice

Q：哪本書好？

哪本书好？

Nǎ běn shū hǎo ？

Which book is good?

A：________________。

2.

Q：那家餐廳怎麼樣？

那家餐厅怎么样？

Nà jiā cāntīng zěnmeyàng ？

How is that restaurant?

A：口味很道地，也不太貴。

口味很道地，也不太贵。

Kǒuwèi hěn dàodì，yě bú tài guì。

Their flavor is very authentic and it's not too expensive.

Practice

Q：這件衣服怎麼樣？

这件衣服怎么样？

Zhè jiàn yīfú zěnmeyàng ？

A：________________。

3.

Q：你去過那家餐廳嗎？

你去过那家餐厅吗？

Nǐ qù guò nà jiā cāntīng ma ？

Have you ever been to that restaurant?

A：a. 沒有，我第一次去。

没有，我第一次去。

Méiyǒu，wǒ dì yī cì qù。

Negative: No. This is my first time going there.

b. 對，我去過。

对，我去过。

Dùi，wǒ qùguò。

Positive: Yes, I have been there.

Practice

Q：你去過中國嗎？

你去过中国吗？

Nǐ qùguò Zhōngguó ma ？

Have you ever been to China?

A：________________。

II. EXERCISE

1. Complete the following dialogue:

A：那家餐廳好嗎？

那家餐厅好吗？

Nà jiā cāntīng hǎo ma ？

B：________。

A：________？

B：有一點兒貴，不好吃。

有一点儿贵，不好吃。

Yǒuyīdiǎnr guì，bùhǎochī。

A：你吃過宮保雞丁嗎？

你吃过宫保鸡丁吗？

Nǐ chī guò Gōngbǎojīdīng ma ？

B：________。

2. Tasks

Skit:

Student A: You are a customer who has never been to a Chinese restaurant before. This will be your first time trying Chinese food.

Student B: You are the waiter at the restaurant. Please introduce the customer to the food on the menu.

III. SUPPLEMENTARY EXPLANATION

1. 味道（5 flavor）

Taste	甜 甜	鹹 咸	苦 苦	酸 酸	辣 辣

Pinyin	tián	xián	kǔ	suān	là
English	sweet	salty	bitter	sour	spicy

2. 時間

Time	點 点	分 分	秒 秒	刻 刻
Pinyin	diǎn	fēn	miǎo	kè
English	o'clock	minute	second	a quarter

IV. CULTURAL NOTES

1. Delicious Chinese food（美味中國菜）

There is a wide variety of Chinese food, which can be very complex as different regions have dishes with their own unique taste.

The staple foods in northern China, by the Yellow River basin, are wheat based, but staple foods in Northeast China, by the Yangtze River, and more southern parts of China are rice-based.

In terms of taste and flavor, central and western provinces, such as Sichuan, Hunan, Yunnan, and Shanxi, are known for their spicy dishes. Shanxi province, which is west of Beijing, is known for their sour dishes, Shanghai is known for their relatively salty dishes, and Cantonese dishes are salty and sweet. Taiwanese dishes, on the other hand, are very diverse due to the influences of immigrants from many parts of China. Taiwanese dishes are described as relatively light.

The earliest Chinese immigrants in the United States are from Guangdong; therefore, Cantonese cuisine is most common in Chinatown. There's a Chinese saying referring to extreme food-lovers that goes, "You will eat anything that has four legs except for tables, and will eat anything in the sea that swims except for submarines." Cantonese dishes are known for being diverse and abundant, making the eating and ordering process more complicated yet fun.

When going to a Chinese restaurant, you should learn about the origin of the dishes and be open to trying things you have never eaten before.

2.Chopsticks（筷子）

Chopsticks are one of the more unique forms of tableware you can find in East Asia that has its origin in China. They were the perfect way to get a hot morsel of food from the bowl to your mouth without injury. Chopsticks are typically made from bamboo or wood, but there are even chopsticks made of gold, ivory, and of course plastic.

Because meats and vegetables are generally diced into small pieces while cooking a meal, there is no need for a fork or knife during a typical Chinese meal. Becoming proficient in chopsticks is no easy task for someone who hasn't grown up using them, especially when trying to grab noodles, or the ever-elusive peanut. Mastering chopsticks is more than just knowing how to use them; there is even certain etiquette that goes along with using them that we should all be aware of. For example, picking through food on a plate; picking up and then putting back down food; or "fighting someone with chopsticks" (crossing one's chopsticks with someone else's) are all considered very rude table manners, and should be avoided at all costs. When not using one's chopsticks they should rest flat on the table, on top of the bowl, or in a special chopstick holder found on the table. And one should never stick their chopsticks straight into a bowl of rice; that is considered taboo in Chinese culture. In Taiwan, a typically dinner table will also have a set of serving chopsticks, which everyone uses to put food into their own individual bowls. You don't want to be to slow serving yourself food either; otherwise you'll make others at the table wait, so being good at chopsticks is an important necessity of good table manners.

第八章
UNIT 8

Your photos are interesting.

你的照片真有趣

Warm Up Activities

1. In what ways do you like to communicate with your friends? (ex. email)
2. In your country, are there more and more people spending time checking their smart phones in public?
3. In your opinion, what are some good and bad things about social networking sites?

LESSON 1

STORY

Mark, Jennifer, Jeff, Linda, Maria, and Lin are sharing their photos online. Linda took a lot of pictures during the Kungfu Club fundraising activities and posted them online. Lin happens to be online when Linda is uploading the photos. They begin to chat.

DIALOGUE

Lin：這張照片眞有趣！
這张照片真有趣！
Zhè zhāng zhàopiàn zhēn yǒuqù ！

Linda：是啊！大家看起來好高興！
是啊！大家看起来好高兴！
Shì a ！ Dàjiā kànqǐlái hǎo gāoxìng ！

Lin：你看了 Mark 的照片嗎？
你看了 Mark 的照片吗？
Nǐ kàn le Mark de zhàopiàn ma ？

Linda：還沒，怎麼了？
还没，怎么了？
Háiméi，zěnme le ？

Lin：他有新女朋友了，很漂亮！
他有新女朋友了，很漂亮！
Tā yǒu xīn nǚpéngyǒu le，hěn piàoliàng ！

> Lin: This photo is really interesting.
> Linda: Yes, everyone looks so happy.
> Lin: Have you seen Mark's new photos yet?
> Linda: Not yet. What's up?
> Lin: He's got a new girlfriend. She is really pretty!

DISCUSSION

1. Where are Linda and Lin?
2. How did Lin find out about Mark's new girlfriend?

VOCABULARY

	Traditional Characters	Simplified Characters	Pinyin	English
1	張ㄓㄤ	张	zhāng	(MW) measure word for pieces of paper
2	照ㄓㄠˋ片ㄆㄧㄢˋ	照片	zhàopiàn	(N) photos
3	有ㄧㄡˇ趣ㄑㄩˋ	有趣	yǒuqù	(SV) interesting
4	好ㄏㄠˇ	好	hǎo	(Adv) so
5	高ㄍㄠ興ㄒㄧㄥˋ	高兴	gāoxìng	(SV) happy
6	看ㄎㄢˋ	看	kàn	(V) to see, to view
7	新ㄒㄧㄣ	新	xīn	(SV) new
8	女ㄋㄩˇ朋ㄆㄥˊ友ㄧㄡˇ	女朋友	nǚpéngyǒu	(N) girlfriend
9	女ㄋㄩˇ	女	nǚ	female
10	漂ㄆㄧㄠˋ亮ㄌㄧㄤˋ	漂亮	piàoliàng	(Adv) pretty

EXPRESSION

	Traditional Characters	Simplified Characters	Pinyin	English
1	看起來	看起来	kànqǐlái	look
2	還沒	还没	háiméi	not yet
3	怎麼了？	怎么了？	zěnme le	what's up?

GRAMMAR

1. N + 看起來 + SV
N + kànqǐlái + SV

Example:

他看起來很好。

他看起来很好。

Tā kànqǐlái hěn hǎo。

He looks great.

2. V + 了 + N
V + le + N

Example:

你看了他的照片嗎？

你看了他的照片吗？

Nǐ kàn le tā de zhàopiàn ma ？

Have you seen his photos?

LESSON 2

STORY

Maria likes Chinese food, so she took some cooking lessons with a Chinese teacher at the Chinese Kitchen in her community. Maria's personal homepage has a lot of links to websites with Chinese recipes . Tonight, Jeff runs into Maria online and starts chatting with her.

DIALOGUE

Jeff：Hi ！中國菜看起來眞好吃！你可以教我嗎？
Hi ！中国菜看起来真好吃！你可以教我吗？
Hi！Zhōngguócài kànqǐlái zhēn hǎochī！Nǐ kěyǐ jiāo wǒ ma？

Maria：你喜歡做菜嗎？
你喜欢做菜吗？
Nǐ xǐhuān zuòcài ma ？

Jeff：很喜歡，我很想學做中國菜。
很喜欢，我很想学做中国菜。
Hěn xǐhuān，wǒ hěn xiǎng xué zuò Zhōngguócài。

Maria：好啊！可是有一點兒難。
好啊！可是有一点儿难。
Hǎo a ！ Kěshì yǒuyìdiǎnér nán。

Jeff：沒問題，我很聰明。
没问题，我很聪明。
Méi wèn tí，wǒ hěn cōngmíng。

Jeff: Hi, that Chinese food looks so delicious. Can you teach me?
Maria: Do you like to cook?
Jeff: Yeah, a lot. I really want to learn to cook Chinese food.
Maria: O.K. It's a little bit difficult, though.
Jeff: No problem. I'm very smart.

DISCUSSION

1. Does Jeff like to cook?
2. What does Jeff want to learn to do?

VOCABULARY

	Traditional Characters	Simplified Characters	Pinyin	English
1	教	教	jiāo	(V) teach
2	做菜	做菜	zuòcài	(V) to cook
3	學	学	xué	(V) to learn
4	有一點兒	有一点儿	yǒuyīdiǎnr	(Adv) a little bit
5	難	难	nán	(SV) difficult
6	聰明	聪明	cōngmíng	(SV) smart

TERM

	Traditional Characters	Simplified Characters	Pinyin	English
1	中國菜	中国菜	Zhōngguócài	Chinese food

GRAMMAR

1. Someone + 可以 + V + N + 嗎？
Someone + kěyǐ + V + N + ma?

Example:

你可以教我嗎？
你可以教我吗？
Nǐ kěyǐ jiāo wǒ ma ？
Can you teach me?

2. 有一點兒 + SV
yǒuyìdiǎnér + SV

Example:

中文有一點兒難。
中文有一点儿难。
Zhōngwén yǒuyìdiǎnér nán。
Chinese is a little difficult.

I. PRACTICE

1.

Q：我看起來怎麼樣？
我看起来怎么样？
Wǒ kànqǐlái zěnmeyàng ？
How do I look?

A：你看起來很好。
你看起来很好。
Nǐ kànqǐlái hěn hǎo。
You look great.

Practice

Q：這件衣服看起來怎麼樣？

这件衣服看起来怎么样？

Zhè jiàn yīfú kànqǐlái zěnmeyàng ？

How do these clothes look?

A：________________。

2.

Q：你看了他的照片嗎？

你看了他的照片吗？

Nǐ kàn le tā de zhàopiàn ma ？

Have you seen his photos yet?

A：a. 還沒。

還没。

Háiméi。

Negative: Not yet.

b. 看了。

看了。

Kàn le。

Positive: Yes, I have.

Practice

Q：你吃飯了嗎？

你吃饭了吗？

Nǐ chī fàn le ma ？

Have you eaten yet?

A：________________。

3.

Q：你可以教我做中國菜嗎？

你可以教我做中国菜吗？

Nǐ kěyǐ jiāo wǒ zuò Zhōngguócài ma ？

Can you teach me how to cook Chinese food?

A：好啊，可是有一點兒難。

好啊，可是有一点儿难。

Hǎo a，kěshì yǒuyìdiǎnér nán。

Yes, but it is a little difficult.

Practice

Q：你可以教我中文嗎？

你可以教我中文吗？

Nǐ kěyǐ jiāo wǒ Zhōngwén ma ？

Can you teach me Mandarin?

A：＿＿＿＿＿＿＿＿。

II. EXERCISE

1. Complete the following dialogue:

A：＿＿＿＿＿？

B：這雙鞋子看起來很漂亮。

这双鞋子看起来很漂亮。

Zhè shuāng xiézi kànqǐlái hěn piàoliàng。

A：你可以教我做中國菜嗎？

你可以教我做中国菜吗？

Nǐ kěyǐ jiāo wǒ zuò Zhōngguócài ma ？

B：＿＿＿＿＿。

2. Tasks

Please introduce a Chinese restaurant by showing everyone the photos of the menu and food that you ordered.

III. SUPPLEMENTARY EXPLANATION

1. 形容詞對比

Adjective	漂亮 漂亮	難 难	聰明 聪明
Pinyin	piàoliàng	nán	cōngmíng
English	pretty	different	smart
Adjective	醜 丑	容易 / 簡單 容易 / 简单	笨 / 呆 笨 / 呆
Pinyin	chǒu	róngyì / jiǎndān	bèn / dāi
English	ugly	easy	stupid, dumb

IV. CULTURAL NOTES

1. Social Network（社群網路）

Similar to the U.S., Facebook is the primary social networking site used in Taiwan. Over fifty percent of the population (about 13 million people) use Facebook. China, on the other hand, uses The Renren Network, which is a remake of Facebook that is very popular among college students in China, with over 30 million monthly users (Note: Facebook is prohibited in China so far). As for online messengers on mobike phone, Taiwanese people mainly use Line and What's App and people from Mainland China use Weixin (微信) Messenger to communicate with friends. Also, a site similar to Twitter, called Weibo, is widely used in China for celebrities to connect with their fans.

2. Yin Yang in Chinese Dishes（陰陽與中國菜）

Yin Yang represents polar opposite concepts and properties, such as male (yáng) and female (yīn), hot (yáng) and cold (yīn). Yin Yang is the heart of Chinese philosophy and is manifested in Chinese dishes. For instance, stir-frying beef with bell peppers or mixing sweet and sour flavors in dishes. Also, ingredients with warm properties should be consumed with cool properties to achieve a healthy balanced diet. If you are suffering from heartburn, traditional Chinese doctors believe that you have consumed too much spicy food because it contains yang properties. To recover from it, you will be advised to drink herbal tea, which has yin properties to balance out the yin and yang in your body.

In addition, there are cooking methods that demonstrate yin and yang qualities. Yin methods include poaching, boiling, and steaming, whereas Yang methods are deep-frying, roasting, and stir-frying.

	Hot	Warm	Neutral	Cool	Cold
Meat	Lamb	Beef	Chicken Pigeon Pork	Duck	Crab
Vegetables	Red chilli	Ginger Green pepper Onion	Carrot Cauliflower Yam	Broccoli Cabbage Celery	Mung bean Sprout Cucumber
Fruits	Lychee	Peach	Pineapple Grape	Apple Orange Pear Mango	Banana Watermelon
Grains and nuts	Sesame seed	Walnut Peanut Sunflower seed	Brown rice White rice	Almond Coconut Wheat flour	Mung bean

source: Compiled from [6, 9]

第九章
UNIT 9

What color do you like?
你喜歡什麼顏色？

Warm Up Activities

1. What color do you like? Why?
2. Do colors carry any special meanings in your culture?

LESSON 1

STORY

The community center near the school will have a series of activities for Chinese Week. The Kung Fu Club was invited to perform. Jennifer and Jeff are working on their costumes for the performance. Mark knows that Linda is very interested in fashion design so he asks her to join them. The following coversation is a discussion of the color for the Kung Fu Club uniform.

DIALOGUE

Jennifer：這兩個顏色，你覺得哪一個好？
这两个颜色，你觉得哪一个好？
Zhè liǎng ge yánsè，nǐ juéde nǎ yí ge hǎo ？

Jeff：白色的比較好看。
白色的比较好看。
Báisè de bǐjiào hǎokàn。

Mark：黑色的比較酷。Linda，你覺得呢？
黑色的比较酷。Linda，你觉得呢？
Hēisè de bǐjiào kù。Linda，nǐ juéde ne ？

Linda：我覺得都好看，可是白色的比較合適。
我觉得都好看，可是白色的比较合适。
Wǒ juéde dōu hǎokàn，kěshì báisè de bǐjiào héshì。

Jennifer：好。我們選白色。
好。我们选白色。
Hǎo。Wǒmen xuǎn báisè。

Jennifer: Which one of the two colors do you think is better?
Jeff: White is better.
Mark: Black is cooler. Linda, what do you think?
Linda: I think both look nice, but white is more appropriate.
Jennifer: O.K. We'll go with white.

DISCUSSION

1. What color does Jeff like? Why?
2. What color does Mark like? Why?

VOCABULARY

	Traditional Characters	Simplified Characters	Pinyin	English
1	顏色	颜色	yánsè	(N) color
2	覺得	觉得	juéde	(V) to feel
3	白色	白色	báisè	(N) white color
4	比較	比较	bǐjiào	(Adv) more
5	好看	好看	hǎokàn	(SV) good looking
6	黑色	黑色	hēisè	(N) black color
7	酷	酷	kù	(SV) cool
8	合適	合适	héshì	(SV) appropriate
9	選	选	xuǎn	(V) to choose

GRAMMAR

1. 哪 + NU + MW
Nǎ + NU + MW

Example:

哪一件？

哪一件？

Nǎ yí jiàn ？

Which one?

2. Noun + 比較 + SV
Noun + bǐjiào + SV

Example:

黑色的比較好看。

黑色的比较好看。

Hēisè de bǐjiào hǎokàn。

Black is better looking.

LESSON 2

STORY

Maria's sister, Olivia, is going to a Chinese friend's wedding. She wants to wear a cheongsam, a Chinese style formal dress, but does not know where to get one. Maria is asking Linda for help and Linda recommends a clothing store in China town. This afternoon, Maria, Olivia, and Linda go to this store and discuss the size and price of the dress with the clerk.

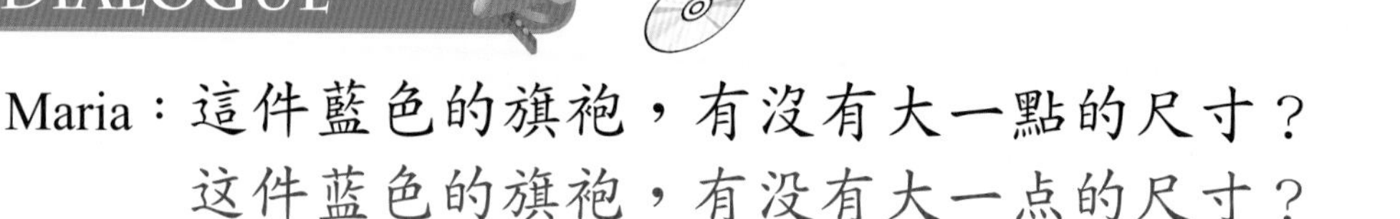

Maria：這件藍色的旗袍，有沒有大一點的尺寸？
这件蓝色的旗袍，有没有大一点的尺寸？
Zhè jiàn lánsè de qípáo，yǒuméiyǒu dà yīdiǎn de chǐcùn ？

Clerk：沒有了，可是綠色和紫色的都有。
没有了，可是绿色和紫色的都有。
Méiyǒu le，kěshì lǜsè hé/hàn zǐsè de dōu yǒu。

Linda：綠色的很適合你姊姊！
绿色的很适合你姊姊！
Lǜsè de hěn shìhé nǐ jiějie ！

Maria：請你給我大號綠色的，我們穿穿看。
请你给我大号绿色的，我们穿穿看。
Qǐng nǐ gěi wǒ dàhào lǜsè de，wǒmen chuānchuānkàn。

(Olivia tries this one and it fits perfectly.)

Maria：請問多少錢？
请问多少钱?
Qǐngwèn duōshǎo qián ？

Clerk：這件旗袍一百九十九元。
这件旗袍一百九十九元。
Zhè jiàn qípáo yìbǎijiǔshíjiǔ yuán。

Maria：太貴了！
太贵了！
Tài guì le ！

Maria: Do you have the blue one in a larger size?
Clerk: No, but we have them in green and purple.
Linda: Green really suits you!
Maria: Could I please see the green one in a larger size?
We'll try it on and see.
(Olivia tries this one and it fits perfectly.)
Maria: How much is it?
Clerk: This one is one hundred and ninty-nine dollars.
Maria: It's too expensive!

DISCUSSION

1. What clothes does Olivia want to buy?
2. What's the color of the clothes that Olivia tries on?
3. How much are the clothes?

VOCABULARY

	Traditional Characters	Simplified Characters	Pinyin	English
1	件	件	jiàn	(MW) measure word for clothes
2	藍色	蓝色	lánsè	(N) blue
3	大	大	dà	big
4	尺寸	尺寸	chǐcùn	(N) size
5	綠色	绿色	lǜsè	(N) green
6	紫色	紫色	zǐsè	(N) purple
7	適合	适合	shìhé	(SV) suitable
8	給	给	gěi	(V) to give

	Traditional Characters	Simplified Characters	Pinyin	English
9	號	号	hào	(N) size number
10	多少	多少	duōshǎo	how much
11	錢	钱	qián	money
12	元／塊	元 / 块	yuán/ kuài	(N) dollar

	Traditional Characters	Simplified Characters	Pinyin	English
1	旗袍	旗袍	qípáo	cheongsam

EXPRESSION

	Traditional Characters	Simplified Characters	Pinyin	English
1	大／中／小號（L, M, S）	大／中／小号	dà/zhōng/xiǎo hào	large/medium/small sizes

GRAMMAR

1. 有沒有 + NU ／大中小 + 號 + N
Yǒuméiyǒu + NU/dà zhōng xiǎo + hào + N

Example:

Q：有沒有 7 號的鞋子？
有没有 7 号的鞋子？
Yǒuméiyǒu qī hào de xiézi ？
Do you have size seven shoes?

A：有沒有大號的衣服？
有没有大号的衣服？
Yǒuméiyǒu dà hào de yīfú ？
Do you have clothes in large?

2. N1 + N2 + (someone) + 都 + V
N1 + N2 + (someone) + dōu + V

Example:

中文、英文，我都會說。
中文、英文，我都会说。
Zhōngwén、Yīngwén，wǒ dōu huì shuō。
Mandarin and English, I can speak both.

3. 請 + 給 + someone + NU + MW + N
Qǐng + gěi + someone + NU + MW + N

Example:

請給我一件衣服。
请给我一件衣服。
Qǐng gěi wǒ yí jiàn yīfú。
Please give me a piece of clothing.

4. V + same V + 看
V + same V + kàn

Example:

穿穿看。

穿穿看。

Chuānchuānkàn。

Try it on.

寫寫看。

写写看。

Xiěxiěkàn。

Write this.

I. PRACTICE

1.

Q：你覺得哪一個顏色好看？

你觉得哪一个颜色好看？

Nǐ juéde nǎ yí ge yánsè hǎokàn ？

Which color do you think is better looking?

A：黑色的比較好看。

黑色的比较好看。

Hēisè de bǐjiào hǎokàn。

The black one is better looking.

Practice

Q：你覺得哪一件衣服好看？

你觉得哪一件衣服好看？

Nǐ juéde nǎ yí jiàn yīfú hǎokàn ？

Which clothes do you think are better looking?

A：＿＿＿＿＿＿＿＿。

2.

Q：黑色、白色，哪一個好看？

黑色、白色，哪一个好看？

Hēisè、báisè，nǎ yí ge hǎokàn ？

Which is better looking? Black or white?

A：黑色、白色，都好看。

黑色、白色，都好看。

Hēisè、báisè，dōu hǎokàn。

Both black and white are good looking.

Practice

Q：今天、明天，哪一天有空？

今天、明天，哪一天有空？

Jīntiān、míngtiān，nǎ yì tiān yǒukòng ？

Which day do you have free time, today or tomorrow?

A：________________。

3.

Q：有沒有 6 號的尺寸？

有没有 6 号的尺寸？

Yǒuméiyǒu liù hào de chǐcùn ？

Do you have a size 6?

A：藍色的沒有了，綠色的有。

蓝色的没有了，绿色的有。

Lánsè de méiyǒu le，lǜsè de yǒu。

We don’t have it in blue, but we have green.

Practice

Q：有沒有中號的尺寸？
有没有中号的尺寸？
Yǒuméiyǒu zhōng hào de chǐcùn ？
Do you have this in a medium?
A：＿＿＿＿＿＿＿＿。

4.

Q：這件衣服，多少錢？
这件衣服，多少钱？
Zhè jiàn yīfú，duōshǎo qián ？
These clothes, how much are they?

A：一百九十九元（塊）。
一百九十九元（块）。
Yìbǎijiǔshíjiǔ yuán(kuài)。
One hundred and ninety-nine dollars.

Practice

Q：這雙鞋，多少錢？
这双鞋，多少钱？
Zhè shuāng xié duōshǎo qián ？
A：＿＿＿＿＿＿＿＿。

II. EXERCISE

1. Complete the following dialogue:

A：你覺得哪一個顏色好看？
你觉得哪一个颜色好看？
Nǐ juéde nǎ yí ge yánsè hǎokàn ？
B：＿＿＿＿＿＿。

A：Linda、Jennifer，哪一個漂亮？

Linda、Jennifer，哪一个漂亮？

Linda、Jennifer，nǎ yí ge piàoliàng ？

B：__________。

A：__________？

B：這件衣服只有小號的尺寸。

这件衣服只有小号的尺寸。

Zhè jiàn yīfú zhǐyǒu S hào de chǐcùn。

A：__________？

B：這件衣服 39.5 元。

这件衣服 39.5 元。

Zhè jiàn yīfú sānshíjiǔdiǎnwǔ yuán。

2. Tasks

Skit

Student A: You are the clerk in the clothing store.

Student B: You are a customer who is trying to buy a dress and shoes for the school prom.

III. SUPPLEMENTARY EXPLANATIONS

1. 酷酷 kù is the Chinese transliteration for "Cool." It's a common phrase among the younger generation.
2. The complete expression for "$99.90" is 九十九塊九毛錢 九十九块九毛钱，but it can be abbreviated as 九十九塊九 九十九块九 .
3. Topic + Comment sentence

   The Noun in the beginning of the sentence is not the subject of the sentence, but an object to be commented on. This is a common Mandarin sentence pattern.

黑色、白色都好看 黑色、白色都好看 Literally: black and white, they are both good-looking.

這雙鞋，多少錢？这双鞋，多少钱？Literally: this pair of shoes, how much?

4. 其他常用顏色

Color	紅 红	黃 黄	棕 棕	灰 灰	金 金	粉紅 粉红
Pinyin	hóng	huáng	zōng	huī	jīn	fěnhóng
English	red	yellow	brown	grey	golden/gold	pink

IV. CULTURAL NOTES

1. Cultural Colors（不同文化的顏色內涵）

Colors are more than just how different light wavelengths are reflected and perceived by the human eye. Colors also represent the viewpoints of cultures and societies all around the world, and while sometimes these viewpoints are the same between cultures, there are other times when these colors can represent very different things. In the U.S. for example, the color red carries a sense of energy, excitement, even danger. When combined with green one can't help but think of Christmas. In China, however, the color red is very auspicious, representing good fortune, luck, and long life.

While a western bride is expected to have a beautiful white wedding gown to celebrate purity and cleanliness, the color white in traditional Chinese culture is often reserved for death and mourning, and humility, with brides wearing red on their wedding day. While some of these cultural associations are slowly changing in our more connected and globalized world, colors still represent many different things to different cultures. What kinds of things do you associate with the colors red and white?

2. Evolution of Chinese Fashion（華人服裝的變遷）

Chinese fashion has evolved with the popular ideologies of the time. In the 1930s, a long body-hugging Chinese dress, called the " 旗 袍 qípáo", was very fashionable in China and was worn by many upper class Chinese women. From 1949 to 1964, due China and Russia having strong ties, cadre uniforms and Russian "bulaji" skirts were the popular outfit during this period. From 1966 to 1976, during the Cultural Revolution, Mao uniforms became very popular. These uniforms are typically green, grey, and blue and made everyone appear ordinary and uniform. From 1978 to 1989, with the influence of foreign investors arriving in China, the country started embracing Western fashion. There was a rise in the popularity of western suits. In the 1990s, Chinese women started to diversify their outfits, wearing mini skirts and suit dresses, which reflects their more open-minded mindset. Finally, within the last decade, China has finally demonstrated their eagerness to express their own personality and steer from conservative trends; even girls wearing bikinis can be seen at the beach.

第十章
UNIT 10

What happened to Linda?

Linda怎麼了？

Warm Up Activities

1. What do you usually do when you catch a cold?
2. Is it expensive to go to the doctors in your country?

LESSON 1

STORY

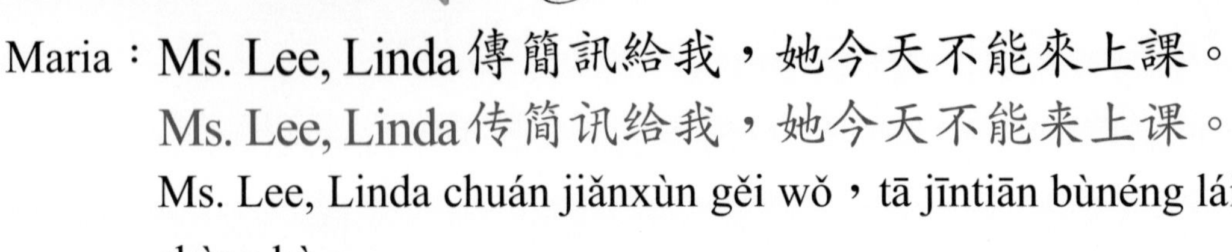

Linda caught a cold while she was practicing cheerleading yesterday. She had a fever and a sore throat when she got home so she sent a text message to Maria telling her she is sick and won't be able to go to school today. In Mandarin class, Maria told the teacher that Linda caught a cold.

DIALOGUE

Maria：Ms. Lee, Linda傳簡訊給我，她今天不能來上課。
Ms. Lee, Linda传简讯给我，她今天不能来上课。
Ms. Lee, Linda chuán jiǎnxùn gěi wǒ，tā jīntiān bùnéng lái shàng kè。

Ms. Lee：她怎麼了？
她怎么了？
Tā zěnme le ？

Maria：她不舒服，大概感冒了。
她不舒服，大概感冒了。
Tā bù shūfú，dàgài gǎnmào le。

Mark：她看醫生了嗎？
她看医生了吗？
Tā kàn yīshēng le ma ？

Maria：不知道。應該在家休息。
不知道。应该在家休息。
Bùzhīdào。Yīnggāi zài jiā xiūxí。

Maria: Ms. Lee, Linda sent me a text message saying she wouldn't be able to come to class today.
Ms. Lee: What happened to her?
Maria: She is not feeling well. I think she caught a cold.
Mark: Did she see a doctor?
Maria: I don't know. She's probably at home resting.

DISCUSSION

1. Why is Linda missing class?
2. How did Maria find out that Linda is sick?

VOCABULARY

	Traditional Characters	Simplified Characters	Pinyin	English
1	傳	传	chuán	(V) send
2	簡訊	简讯	jiǎnxùn	(N) text message
3	給	给	gěi	(Prep) to
4	能	能	néng	(AV) to be able to,can
5	上課	上课	shàng kè	(V) to have class
6	舒服	舒服	shūfú	(SV) comfortable
7	大概	大概	dàgài	(Adv) perhaps, most likely
8	感冒	感冒	gǎnmào	(V) to catch a cold
9	醫生	医生	yīshēng	(N) doctor
10	應該	应该	yīnggāi	(AV) should
11	休息	休息	xiūxí	(V) to rest

EXPRESSION

	Traditional Characters	Simplified Characters	Pinyin	English
1	怎麼了？	怎么了？	zěnme le	what happened?

GRAMMAR

1. Someone + V + 了
Someone + V + le

Example:

我看醫生了。

我看医生了。

Wǒ kàn yīshēng le。

I went to see a doctor.

我感冒了。

我感冒了。

Wǒ gǎnmào le。

I caught a cold.

LESSON 2

STORY

Jeff got up and found himself with a headache. His throat was itching, and he kept coughing. Jeff's mom took his temperature and discovered out that Jeff has a fever. She told Jeff that since he has the flu, he should not go to school today. Jeff calls Jennifer to tell her that he won't be able to join the kung fu practice this afternoon. Jennifer is trying to say something to make him feel better.

DIALOGUE

Jeff：Jennifer，我今天不能去練習了。
Jennifer，我今天不能去练习了。
Jennifer，wǒ jīntiān bùnéng qù liànxí le。

Jennifer：爲什麼？你生病了嗎？
为什么？你生病了吗？
Wèishénme ？ Nǐ shēngbìng le ma ？

Jeff：嗯，我頭很痛，好像發燒了，覺得不舒服。對不起。
嗯，我头很痛，好像发烧了，觉得不舒服。对不起。
En，wǒ tóu hěn tòng，hǎoxiàng fāshāo le，juéde bù shūfú。Duìbùqǐ。

Jennifer：沒關係，你在家休息吧，要多喝水。
没关系，你在家休息吧，要多喝水。
Méiguānxi，nǐ zài jiā xiūxí ba，yào duō hē shuǐ。

Jeff：好的，再見。
好的，再见。
Hǎode，zàijiàn。

Jeff: Jennifer, I can't go to practice today.
Jennifer: Why? Are you sick?
Jeff: Yes, I have a headache and I think I have a fever. I am really not feeling very well. Sorry.
Jennifer: It's O.K. You can stay home and rest. Be sure to drink lots of water.
Jeff: All right. Bye.

DISCUSSION

1. What happened to Jeff?
2. What did Jennifer say?

VOCABULARY

	Traditional Characters	Simplified Characters	Pinyin	English
1	練ㄌㄧㄢˋ習ㄒㄧˊ	练习	liànxí	(V) pratice
2	生ㄕㄥ病ㄅㄧㄥˋ	生病	shēngbìng	(SV) to be sick
3	頭ㄊㄡˊ	头	tóu	(N) head
4	痛ㄊㄨㄥˋ	痛	tòng	(N) ache
5	好ㄏㄠˇ像ㄒㄧㄤˋ	好像	hǎoxiàng	(Adv) seems like

	Traditional Characters	Simplified Characters	Pinyin	English
6	發燒	发烧	fāshāo	(V) running a fever
7	要	要	yào	(Adv) have to
8	多	多	duō	(Adv) more
9	喝	喝	hē	(V) to drink
10	水	水	shuǐ	(N) water

EXPRESSION

	Traditional Characters	Simplified Characters	Pinyin	English
1	為什麼？	为什么？	wèishénme	why?
2	沒關係	没关系	méiguānxi	it's O.K.
3	好的	好的	hǎode	all right
4	再見	再见	zàijiàn	good bye

GRAMMAR

1. 不 + Verb + 了

bú + Verb + le

Example:

不去練習了。

不去练习了。

Bú qù liànxí le。

Not to go to practice

2. 好像 + V + 了

hǎoxiàng + V + le

Example:

好像生病了。

好像生病了。

Hǎoxiàng shēngbìng le。

[someone] seems to have caught a cold.

他好像回家了。

他好像回家了。

Tā hǎoxiàng huí jiā le。

He seems to have headed home.

3. Someone + 要 + 多 + V

Someone + yào + duō + V

Example:

你要多喝水。

你要多喝水。

Nǐ yào duō hē shuǐ。

You have to drink more water.

你要多練習。

你要多练习。

Nǐ yào duō liànxí。

You have to practice more.

I. PRACTICE

1.

Q：Mark 怎麼了？

Mark 怎么了？

Mark zěnme le ？

How is Mark? (What happened to Mark?)

A：他不舒服。

他不舒服。

Tā bù shūfú。

He is not feeling well.

Practice

Q：你怎麼了？

你怎么了？

Nǐ zěnme le ？

What happened to you?

A：＿＿＿＿＿＿＿＿。

2.

Q：Linda 生病了嗎？

Linda 生病了吗？

Linda shēngbìng le ma ？

Is Linda sick?

A：她生病了。

她生病了。

Tā shēngbìng le。

(Positive) She is sick.

她沒生病。

她没生病。

Tā méi shēngbìng。

(Negative) She is not sick.

Practice

Q：你感冒了嗎？

你感冒了吗？

Nǐ gǎnmào le ma ？

Have you caught a cold?

A：________________。

Q：你吃飯了嗎？

你吃饭了吗？

Nǐ chī fàn le ma ？

Have you eaten?

A：________________。

3.

A：我覺得不舒服。

我觉得不舒服。

Wǒ juéde bù shūfú。

I am not feeling well.

B：你要多休息。

你要多休息。

Nǐ yào duō xiūxí。

You have to get some rest.

Practice

A：我頭很痛。

我头很痛。

Wǒ tóu hěn tòng。

I have a terrible headache.

B：你要多__________。

你要多__________。

Nǐ yào duō __________。

You have to __________.

II. EXERCISE

1. Complete the following dialogue:

A：你怎麼了？

你怎么了？

Nǐ zěnme le ？

What happened to you?

B：__________。

A：我不舒服。

我不舒服。

Wǒ bù shūfú。

I am not feeling well.

B：__________。

A：__________。

B：你要多練習。

你要多练习。

Nǐ yào duō liànxí。

You have to practice more.

2. Tasks

Student A: You are a student getting sick. Call your friends and ask them to let the teacher know that you won't be in class.

Student B: You agree to help your friend. Say something to make him/her feel better.

III. SUPPLEMENTARY EXPLANATIONS

1. 生病症狀的說法 Symptoms of diseases

Illness	咳嗽 咳嗽	流鼻水 流鼻水	打噴嚏 打喷嚏	喉嚨痛 喉咙痛	肚子痛 肚子痛
Pinyin	késòu	liú bíshuǐ	dǎ pēntì	hóulóng tòng	dǔzitòng
English	cough	running nose	sneeze	sore throat	stomachache

2. 身體部位的說法 Body parts

Body Parts	臉 脸	眼睛 眼睛	鼻子 鼻子	耳朵 耳朵	嘴巴 嘴巴
Pinyin	liǎn	yǎnjīng	bízi	ěrduo	zuǐbā
English	face	eye(s)	nose	ear(s)	mouth
Body Parts	脖子 脖子	肩膀 肩膀	手／手臂 手／手臂	腿／腳 腿／脚	肌肉 肌肉
Pinyin	bózi	jiānbǎng	shǒu/shǒu bì	tuǐ/jiǎo	jīròu
English	neck	shoulder	hand/arm	leg/foot	muscle(s)

3. When you say "What happened to you?" to someone, it usually looks like something negative happened to that person. For example, he/she maybe sick, angry, or crying.
4. When you add "了了 le" after a verb, it indicates the completion of an action. If you add "了 le" after a stative verb, it indicates change of state. In this lesson, "了了 le" follows a verb so it indicates the completion of an action. For its negative form, add "沒没 méi" in front of the verb. For example:

我沒生病

我沒生病。

Wǒ méi shēngbìng。

I am not sick.

IV. CULTURAL NOTES

1. Traditional Chinese Medicine — acupuncture & massage（中國的傳統醫學療法——針灸與推拿）

Chinese Medicine includes a broad range of medical practices sharing common theoretical concepts, which were developed in China. They are based on more than 2,000 years of tradition, and include various forms of herbal medicine, acupuncture (Zhēnjiǔ), massage (tuīná) and dietary therapy. Diagnostic protocol for Chinese medicine includes: looking, hearing and smelling, questioning, and palpation (feeling). In the first, the physician observes the skin, hair and attitude of the patient. In the second, the physician might analyze the quality of the patient's voice and body odors. Third, the physician will interview the patient, looking for any patterns that might have resulted in the illness. Finally, the physician will gently touch the patient, looking for tender points, especially in the areas along acupuncture meridians. In Chinese medicine, taking the pulse is also extremely important. It is used to derive a diagnosis and a plan for treatment, and is said to help gain a deep understanding of the patient on many levels.

One of the more common elements of Chinese medicine in the west is acupuncture treatment. Acupuncture is a treatment by which thin needles are inserted into acupuncture points in the skin. Massage is popular as well. Massage is a hands-on body treatment where the practitioner may brush, knead, roll, press, and rub areas between each of the joints or acupuncture points in an attempt to open the body's defensive or blocked " 氣 "(qì) getting the energy moving in the meridians and muscles. Acupuncture and massage are two professional treatments that emphasize the operation and balance of chi in one's body, so that recovery from an illness actually comes from the body itself.

2.Dietary Therapy（藥食同源：中國人的食補觀念）

Traditional Chinese Medicine is largely a dietary therapy, taking into consideration that every kind of food has its own unique characteristics, called "the chi of the food". It is classified in four categories: " 熱 "(hot), " 溫 "(warm), " 涼 "(cool), and " 寒 "(cold) by analyzing the body's reactions after eating the food. For example, you will get warm or feel hot after you drink a glass of alcohol or eat a spoon of chili. Chinese medicine, than classifies alcohol and things like chili as a hot foods. Say your body feels like it's on fire in summer time, but after enjoying up a piece of watermelon, your will feel cool and comfortable. In this way, watermelon is classified as a kind of cold food.

Traditional Chinese Medicine also categorizes conditions of the human body and illness into both hot-bodied or cold-bodied.

第十一章

UNIT 11

The Weather in New York.

紐約的天氣

Warm Up Activities

1. How is the summer and winter where you live?
2. How old do you have to be to drive? What kind of transportation do you take most often and why?

LESSON 1

STORY

It is almost mid-term week. Next week, the Mandarin teacher will give the students a quiz. This afternoon, Lin is studying at the library and runs into Jennifer. Jennifer grew up in California and she usually goes back to Shanghai to visit relatives with her mother and her brother, Kevin. Jennifer and Lin start to chat about the differences in weather between America and Asia.

DIALOGUE

Jennifer：上海的夏天很熱，臺灣跟上海一樣吧？
上海的夏天很热，台湾跟上海一样吧？
Shànghǎi de xiàtiān hěn rè，Táiwān gēn Shànghǎi yíyàng ba ？

Lin：臺灣的夏天非常熱，眞受不了！
台湾的夏天非常热，真受不了！
Táiwān de xiàtiān fēicháng rè，zhēn shòubùliǎo ！

Jennifer：你覺得紐約的天氣怎麼樣？
你觉得纽约的天气怎么样？
Nǐ juéde Niǔyuē de tiānqì zěnmeyàng ？

Lin：這裡的冬天比加州冷得多。
这里的冬天比加州冷得多。
Zhèlǐ de dōngtiān bǐ Jiāzhōu lěng de duō。

Jennifer：我比較喜歡冷的地方。我喜歡下雪。
我比较喜欢冷的地方。我喜欢下雪。
Wǒ bǐjiào xǐhuān lěng de dìfāng。Wǒ xǐhuān xià xuě。

Lin：臺北的冬天不下雪，可是常常下雨。
台北的冬天不下雪，可是常常下雨。
Táiběi de dōngtiān bú xià xuě，kěshì chángcháng xià yǔ。

Jennifer: It is really hot during the summer in Shanghai. Taipei is just like Shanghai, right?
Lin: The summer in Taiwan is terribly hot. It's unbearable.
Jennifer: How do you like the weather in New York?
Lin: The winter here is much colder than in California.
Jennifer: I prefer cold weather. I like when it snows.
Lin: It doesn't snow during the winter in Taipei, but it rains a lot.

DISCUSSION

1. How is the summer in Shanghai and Taiwan?
2. Where is it colder in winter? New York or California?

VOCABULARY

	Traditional Characters	Simplified Characters	Pinyin	English
1	夏天	夏天	xiàtiān	(N) summer
2	非常	非常	fēicháng	(Adv) very
3	熱	热	rè	(SV) hot
4	跟	跟	gēn	(P) with
5	一樣	一样	yíyàng	(SV) same
6	真	真	zhēn	(Adv) really
7	天氣	天气	tiānqì	(N) weather
8	冬天	冬天	dōngtiān	(N) winter
9	冷	冷	lěng	(SV) cold
10	下雪	下雪	xià xuě	(V) to snow
11	下雨	下雨	xià yǔ	(V) to rain

TERM

	Traditional Characters	Simplified Characters	Pinyin	English
1	紐約	纽约	Niǔyuē	New York
2	加州	加州	Jiāzhōu	California
3	臺北	台北	Táiběi	Taipei

EXPRESSION

	Traditional Characters	Simplified Characters	Pinyin	English
1	受不了	受不了	shòubùliǎo	unbearable

GRAMMAR

1. N + 跟 + N + 一樣 + SV

N + gēn+ N + yíyàng + SV

Example:

臺北跟上海一樣熱。

台北跟上海一样热。

Táiběi gēn Shànghǎi yíyàng rè。

Taipei is as hot as Shanghai.

2. N + 比 + N + SV + 得多

N + bǐ + N + SV + de + SV

Example:

加州比紐約熱得多。

加州比纽约热得多。

Jiāzhōu bǐ Niǔyuē rè de duō。

California is much hotter than New York.

LESSON 2

STORY

Lin's cousin, Johnny Wang, lives in Taiwan and is two years younger than Lin. This year, Johnny will be a 9th grade student in junior high school. He is preparing for the high school entrance examination that he has to take next year. Johnny wakes up very early in the morning and he has a lot of tests and homework every day. He also has to go to a cram school for extra classes in Math and English. Lin thinks that his cousin seems to have less fun because Johnny does not have any free time to do what he wants to do. In the high school that Lin goes to, he has some homework to do every day, but he still has time to play ball or do other things that interest him. Johnny complains about endless tests to Lin occasionally, but he also says that every student in his grade is going through the same thing. Lin and Johnny chat on the internet sometimes, and Lin also visits Johnny during summer vacation every year. Right now Lin is on Thanksgiving vacation. He and Johnny are chatting about forms of transportation online.

DIALOGUE

Johnny：你平常怎麼上學啊？
你平常怎么上学啊？
Nǐ píngcháng zěnme shàng xué a ？

Lin：我有的時候坐爸爸的車，有時候坐校車。你呢？
我有的时候坐爸爸的车，有时候坐校车。你呢？
Wǒ yǒudeshíhòu zuò bàba de chē，yǒushíhòu zuò xiào chē。Nǐ ne ？

Johnny：我常常坐公車或捷運，下雨天坐計程車。
我常常坐公车或捷运，下雨天坐计程车。
Wǒ chángcháng zuò gōngchē huò jiéyùn，xiàyǔtiān zuò jìchéngchē。

Lin：在紐約計程車很貴，所以我很少坐計程車。
在纽约计程车很贵，所以我很少坐计程车。
Zài Niǔyuē jìchéngchē hěn guì，suǒyǐ wǒ hěn shǎo zuò jìchéngchē。

Johnny：臺北交通很方便，車費也很便宜。
台北交通很方便，车费也很便宜。
Táiběi jiāotōng hěn fāngbiàn，chē fèi yě hěn piányí。

Johnny: How do you usually get to school?
Lin: My father drives me. Sometimes I take the school bus. How about you?
Johnny: I usually take a bus or the subway. On rainy days, I take a taxi.
Lin: Taxi fare is very expensive in New York, so I rarely take a taxi.
Johnny: It's quite easy to get around in Taipei. Transportation fees are also quite cheap.

DISCUSSION

1. How does Lin usually get to school?
2. How does Johnny get to school in Taipei?

	Traditional Characters	Simplified Characters	Pinyin	English
1	平常	平常	píngcháng	(Adv) usually
2	怎麼	怎么	zěnme	(QW) how
3	上學	上学	shàng xué	(V) to go to school
4	坐	坐	zuò	(V) to take
5	車	车	chē	(N) car
6	常常	常常	chángcháng	(Adv) often, usually
7	或	或	huò	(Conj) or
8	很少	很少	hěn shǎo	(Adv) rarely
9	交通	交通	jiāotōng	(N) traffic
10	方便	方便	fāngbiàn	(SV) convenient
11	車費	车费	chē fèi	(N) transportation fee
12	便宜	便宜	piányí	(SV) cheap

TERM

	Traditional Characters	Simplified Characters	Pinyin	English
1	校車	校车	xiào chē	school bus
2	計程車	计程车	jìchéngchē	taxi
3	公車	公车	gōngchē	bus
4	捷運／地鐵	捷运／地铁	jiéyùn/dìtiě	MRT/subway

EXPRESSION

	Traditional Characters	Simplified Characters	Pinyin	English
1	有的時候	有的时候	yǒudeshíhòu	sometimes
2	因為	因为	yīnwèi	because
3	所以	所以	suǒyǐ	so

GRAMMAR

1. Someone + 平常 + V
Someone + píngcháng + V

Example:

我平常在家吃飯。

我平常在家吃饭。

Wǒ píngcháng zài jiā chī fàn。

I usually eat at home.

2. 有的時候 + V
yǒudeshíhòu + V

Example:

我有的時候在家吃飯，有的時候在餐廳吃飯。

我有的时候在家吃饭，有的时候在餐厅吃饭。

Wǒ yǒudeshíhòu zài jiā chī fàn，yǒudeshíhòu zài cāntīng chī fàn。

Sometimes I eat at home. Sometimes I eat out at restaurants.

3. Someone + 常常／很少 + V
Someone + chángcháng/hěn shǎo + V

Example:

我常常坐計程車。

我常常坐计程车。

Wǒ chángcháng zuò jìchéngchē。

I usually take a taxi.

我很少在餐廳吃飯。

我很少在餐厅吃饭。

Wǒ hěn shǎo zài cāntīng chī fàn。

I seldom eat out at restaurants.

I. PRACTICE

1.

Q：紐約的天氣跟臺北一樣嗎？

紐约的天气跟台北一样吗？

Niǔyuē de tiānqì gēn Táiběi yíyàng ma ？

Is the weather in New York the same as Taiwan's?

A：不一樣，紐約比臺北冷。

不一样，纽约比台北冷。

Bù yíyàng，Niǔyuē bǐ Táiběi lěng。

Not the same, New York is colder than Taipei.

Practice

Q：臺北的交通跟紐約一樣嗎？

台北的交通跟纽约一样吗？

Táiběi de jiāotōng gēn Niǔyuē yíyàng ma ？

Is traffic in Taipei the same as traffic in New York?

A：＿＿＿＿＿＿＿＿。

2.

Q：坐計程車比公車貴嗎？

坐计程车比公车贵吗？

Zuò chūzūchē bǐ gōngchē guì ma ？

Is it more expensive to take a taxi than a bus?

A：坐計程車比公車貴得多。

坐计程车比公车贵得多。

Zuò chūzūchē bǐ gōngchē guì de duō。

Taking a taxi is a lot more expensive than taking a bus.

Practice

Q：紐約的東西比臺北的貴嗎？

纽约的东西比台北的贵吗？

Niǔyuē de dōngxi bǐ Táiběi guì ma ？

Are things in New York a lot more expensive than those in Taipei?

A：________________。

3.

Q：你常常在餐廳吃飯嗎？

你常常在餐厅吃饭吗？

Nǐ chángcháng zài cāntīng chī fàn ma ？

Do you usually eat out at restaurants?

A：我很少在餐廳吃飯。

我很少在餐厅吃饭。

Wǒ hěn shǎo zài cāntīng chī fàn。

I rarely eat out at restaurants.

Practice

Q：你常常坐計程車嗎？

你常常坐计程车吗？

Nǐ chángcháng zuò jìchéngchē ma ？

Do you usually take a taxi?

A：＿＿＿＿＿＿＿＿。

II. EXERCISE

1. Complete the following dialogue:

A：紐約的交通怎麼樣？

纽约的交通怎麼样？

Niǔyuē de jiāotōng zěnmeyàng ？

How is traffic in New York?

B：＿＿＿＿＿＿。

A：你常常練習中文嗎？

你常常练习中文吗？

Nǐ chángcháng liànxí Zhōngwén ma ？

Do you practice Mandarin very often?

B：＿＿＿＿＿＿。

A：你为什么不喜欢＿＿＿＿＿＿？

Nǐ wèishénme bù xǐhuān ＿＿＿＿＿＿？

Why don't you like ＿＿＿＿＿＿?

B：因爲＿＿＿＿＿＿。

Yīnwèi ＿＿＿＿＿＿。

Because ＿＿＿＿＿＿.

2. Tasks

Ask your classmates how they got to school today, and tell the class facts such as "Who is faster than whom?" and "Who spend less money on traffic than whom?"

III. SUPPLEMENTARY EXPLANATION

1. 季節 Seasons

Season	春 春	夏 夏	秋 秋	冬 冬	四季 四季
Pinyin	chūn	xià	qiū	dōng	sìjì
English	Spring	Summer	Autumn	Winter	4 Seasons

2. 氣候 Weather

Weather (adj.)	晴 晴	陰 阴	雨 雨	霧 雾	風 风
Pinyin	qíng	yīn	yǔ	wù	fēng
English	Sunny	Cloudy	Raining/Rainy	Foggy	Windy

3. 交通工具 Transportation Vehicles

Traffic	汽車 汽车	機車 机车	飛機 飞机	船 船	自行車／腳踏車 自行车／脚踏车
Pinyin	qìchē	jīchē	fēijī	chuán	zìxíngchē /jiǎotàchē
English	car	motorcycle	airplane	boat	bicycle

4. 費用 Fees

Fee	學費 学费	水／電／瓦斯費 水／电／瓦斯费	住宿費（房租） 住宿费（房租）	生活費 生活费
Pinyin	xué fèi	shuǐ/diàn/wǎsī fèi	zhùsù fèi (fángzū)	shēnghuó fèi
English	tuition	utility fee(s)	rent	living expense(s)

IV. CULTURAL NOTES

1. Umbrellas On Sunny Days（晴天雨天都撐傘的中國人）

When Americans visit Taiwan or China, they would find it amusing how Chinese people would use an umbrella on both rainy and sunny days. From what they've observed, Americans only use umbrellas on rainy days, not when it's sunny out. Americans enjoy sunbathing and achieving tanned skinned because they believe it looks healthier and more attractive.

In China and Taiwan, however, this is not the case. Chinese people don't like to be tanned under sunshine and strive to keep away from the sun because they believe that people can easily tan within a few hours, but it takes more time and effort to maintain white skin. In other words, they believe that using an umbrella when it's sunny out is just as important as when it's raining. On another note, research shows that UV rays can harm the skin and possibly lead to cancer. Therefore, Chinese people are not only using the umbrella on sunny days to maintain white skin, but also to protect themselves from the harmful effects of the sun.

2.Test Culture（亞洲國家的升學制度）

Living in Taiwan or China (even in Japan and South Korea), you may find yourself amazed by the number of cram schools everywhere (after school programs for things like English and Math), that and the fact that students always seem to be studying. Part of this phenomenon stems from the "test culture" that exists in China and Taiwan. From as early as Junior High School (grades 7-9), students take national exams, which will determine where they will attend high school. Even in high school the testing doesn't stop. Many students spend much of their time preparing for the 高考 gāo kǎo, a college prep test know for being even more notorious than the SAT. People with the best grades from these tests generally get into the best schools.

While top Universities in the U.S. certainly talk about good grades, many schools are also looking for excellence in community service, athletics, and other extra-curricular activities. In China and Taiwan, however, top marks in classes and on college entrance exams still take top priority. Right now, there are more than 25 million university students in China, five times the number studying just 10 years ago. Just this year, 9.15 million Chinese seniors took the 高考 gāo kǎo—and for those students, that test alone will ultimately decided where students go to school. Do you think you would be up to such a challenge?

Where are you going for your vacation?

你放假要去哪裡？

Warm Up Activities

1. Please introduce a special holiday in your country. Do you know its origin? What do you typically do to celebrate this holiday?
2. Where would you like to go for a vacation? Why?

LESSON 1

STORY

Jennifer will join the American Youth Kung Fu Competition next week, so recently she has been practicing very diligently. She is spending a lot of time in the Kungfu classroom after classes. The semester is almost over, and Christmas vacation is approaching. With New Year following the Christmas, everyone is about to greet another new year. Mark, Lin, and Jennifer are chatting about their vacation plans in the kung fu classroom.

DIALOGUE

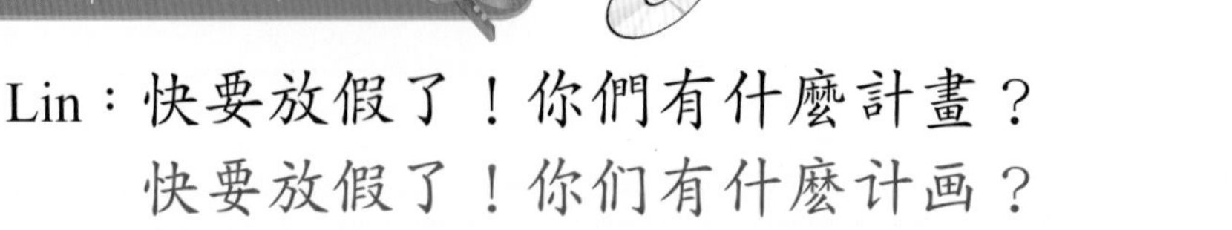

Lin：快要放假了！你們有什麼計畫？
快要放假了！你们有什麽计画？
Kuàiyào fàngjià le ！ Nǐmen yǒu shénme jìhuà ？

Jennifer：我打算跟媽媽回上海看親戚。
我打算跟妈妈回上海看亲戚。
Wǒ dǎsuàn gēn māma huí Shànghǎi kàn qīnqī。

Mark：好棒！我也想去中國旅行。
好棒！我也想去中国旅行。
Hǎo bàng ！ Wǒ yě xiǎng qù Zhōngguó lǚxíng。

Lin：我們去臺灣吧！我們去看臺北的跨年煙火！
我们去台湾吧！我们去看台北的跨年烟火！
Wǒmen qù Táiwān ba ！ Wǒmen qù kàn táiběi de kuànián yānhuǒ ！

Mark：讓我考慮一下！
让我考虑一下！
Ràng wǒ kǎolǜ yíxià ！

> Lin: It's almost winter break. What kind of plans do you have?
> Jennifer: I am planning to go back to Shanghai with my mother to visit my relatives.
> Mark: That sounds great. I would like to travel to China, too.
> Lin: I am going to Taiwan. Let's go to Taiwan to watch the fireworks ushering in the New Year.
> Mark: Let me think about it.

DISCUSSION

1. What is Jennifer's plan?
2. How about Lin?
3. Has Mark decided?

VOCABULARY

	Traditional Characters	Simplified Characters	Pinyin	English
1	快ㄎㄨㄞˋ要ㄧㄠˋ	快要	kuàiyào	(Adv) about to
2	放ㄈㄤˋ假ㄐㄧㄚˋ	放假	fàngjià	(V) to have time off
3	計ㄐㄧˋ畫ㄏㄨㄚˋ	计画	jìhuà	(N,V) plan

	Traditional Characters	Simplified Characters	Pinyin	English
4	打ㄉㄚˇ算ㄙㄨㄢˋ	打算	dǎsuàn	(V) to plan
5	回ㄏㄨㄟˊ	回	huí	(V) to go back
6	親ㄑㄧㄣ戚ㄑㄧ	亲戚	qīnqī	(N) relative
7	旅ㄌㄩˇ行ㄒㄧㄥˊ	旅行	lǚxíng	(V) to travel
8	讓ㄖㄤˋ	让	ràng	(V) to let
9	考ㄎㄠˇ慮ㄌㄩˋ	考虑	kǎolǜ	(V) to think about
10	一ˊ下ㄒㄧㄚˋ	一下	yíxià	(N) a bit, a while

	Traditional Characters	Simplified Characters	Pinyin	English
1	跨ㄎㄨㄚˋ年ㄋㄧㄢˊ煙ㄧㄢ 火ㄏㄨㄛˇ	跨年烟火	kuànián yānhuǒ	fireworks ushering in the new year

EXPRESSION

	Traditional Characters	Simplified Characters	Pinyin	English
1	好ㄏㄠˇ棒ㄅㄤˋ	好棒	hǎo bàng	wonderful

GRAMMAR

1. 快要 + V + 了
kuàiyào + V + 了

Example:

快要上課了。

快要上课了。

Kuàiyào shàng kè le。

Class is about to start.

2. 人 + 跟 + 人 + V
rén +gēn + rén + V

Example:

你跟我去上海旅行。

你跟我去上海旅行。

Nǐ gēn wǒ qù Shànghǎi lǚxíng。

You are traveling to Shanghai with me.

我跟她一起上課。

我跟她一起上课。

Wǒ gēn tā yìqǐ shàng kè。

I am going to class with her.

3. 讓 + someone + V + 一下
Ràng + someone + V + yíxià

Example:

讓我想一下。

让我想一下。

Ràng wǒ xiǎng yíxià。

Let me think about it.

讓我看一下。

让我看一下。

Ràng wǒ kàn yíxià。

Let me take a look.

LESSON 2

STORY

Mark's basketball team won first place in the high school basketball tournament. This afternoon they are celebrating at Mark's house. Jennifer, Jeff, Linda, Maria, and Lin are all there. Linda, Maria, and Jeff are talking about their plans for New Year vacation while they are eating cake. Linda wants to go skiing with her family. Maria will spend her vacation with her relatives. Jeff will help prepare gifts and cookies for people living in the senior apartments.

DIALOGUE

Linda：你們放假要做什麼？
你们放假要做什么？
Nǐmen fàngjià yào zuò shénme ？

Maria：我要和家人度假。你呢？
我要和家人度假。你呢？
Wǒ yào hé/hàn jiārén dùjià。Nǐ ne ？

Linda：還沒決定，可能去滑雪。
还没决定，可能去滑雪。
Háiméi juédìng，kěnéng qù huáxuě。

Jeff：耶誕節的時候，我想做社區服務，要做餅乾給老人公寓的老人。
圣诞节的时候，我想做社区服务，要做饼乾给老人公寓的老人。
Shèngdànjié de shíhòu，wǒ xiǎng zuò shèqū fúwù，yào zuò bǐnggān gěi lǎorén gōngyù de lǎorén。

Linda：真的？我可以去幫忙嗎？
真的？我可以去帮忙吗？
Zhēnde ？ Wǒ kěyǐ qù bāngmáng ma ？

Jeff：當然！
当然！
Dāngrán ！

Linda: What are you guys going to do for the vacation?
Maria: I'll spend time with my family. How about you?
Linda: I haven't decided yet. Maybe we will go to skiing.
Jeff: I want to join the community service program for Christmas. We will make cookies for people living in the senior apartments.
Linda: Really? Can I help?
Jeff: Of course!

DISCUSSION

1. What is Linda going to during the winter break?
2. What will Maria do during the winter break?
3. How about Jeff?

VOCABULARY

	Traditional Characters	Simplified Characters	Pinyin	English
1	度假	度假	dùjià	(V) to be on a vacation
2	決定	决定	juédìng	(V) to decide
3	可能	可能	kěnéng	(Adv) possibly
4	滑雪	滑雪	huáxuě	(V) ski
5	社區	社区	shèqū	(N) community
6	服務	服务	fúwù	(V) to serve
7	餅乾	饼乾	bǐnggān	(N) cookie
8	老人	老人	lǎorén	(N) older people
9	公寓	公寓	gōngyù	(N) apartment
10	幫忙	帮忙	bāngmáng	(V) to help

TERM

	Traditional Characters	Simplified Characters	Pinyin	English
1	聖誕節	圣诞节	Shèngdànjié	Christmas

EXPRESSION

	Traditional Characters	Simplified Characters	Pinyin	English
1	真的（嗎）？	真的（吗）？	zhēnde(ma)	really?
2	當然	当然	dāngrán	of course

GRAMMAR

1. Someone + 可能 + V

Example:

我可能不去上海。

我可能不去上海。

Wǒ kěnéng bú qù Shànghǎi。

I may not be going to Shanghai.

2. Someone + Verb + N + 給 + someone

Example:

我買東西給媽媽。

我买东西给妈妈。

Wǒ mǎi dōngxi gěi māma。

I am buying something for my mom.

I. PRACTICE

1.

Q：你跟誰去超市？
你跟谁去超市？
Nǐ gēn shéi qù chāoshì ？
Whom are you going to the supermarket with?

A：我跟媽媽去超市。
我跟妈妈去超市。
Wǒ gēn māma qù chāoshì。
I am going to the supermarket with my mom.

Practice

Q：你跟誰去滑雪？
你跟谁去滑雪？
Nǐ gēn shéi qù huáxuě ？
Whom are you going skiing with?
A：________________。

2.

Q：你會來我家烤肉嗎？
你会来我家烤肉吗？
Nǐ huì lái wǒ jiā kǎoròu ma ？
Are you coming to my house for a barbecue?

A：我一定會去的。
我一定会去的。
Wǒ yídìng huì qù de。
I am definitely going.

Practice

Q：你明天會去練習嗎？
你明天会去练习吗？
Nǐ míngtiān huì qù liànxí ma ？
Are you going to practice tomorrow?
A：________________。

3.

Q：你買什麼給你媽媽？
你买什麼给你妈妈？
Nǐ mǎi shénme gěi nǐ māma ？
What are you buying for your mom?

A：我買一件衣服給我媽媽。
我买一件衣服给我妈妈。
Wǒ mǎi yí jiàn yīfú gěi wǒ māma。
I will buy clothes for my mom.

Practice

Q：你送什麼給你同學？
你送什麼给你同学？
Nǐ sòng shénme gěi nǐ tóngxué ？
What are you buying for your classmate?
A：________________。

4.

Q：你決定了嗎？
你决定了吗？
Nǐ juédìng le ma ？
Have you decided?

A：還沒，讓我想一下。
還没，让我想一下。
Háiméi，ràng wǒ xiǎng yíxià。
Not yet. Let me think about it.

Practice

Q：你要去哪裡旅行？
你要去哪里旅行？
Nǐ yào qù nǎlǐ lǚxíng ？
Where are you going to travel to?
A：________。

II. EXERCISE

1. Complete the following dialogue:

A：你跟誰________？
你跟谁________？
Nǐ gēn shéi ________？
B：________。

A：你會來幫忙嗎？
你会来帮忙吗？
Nǐ huì lái bāngmáng ma ？
B：________。

A：你買什麼給你朋友？
你买什麼给你朋友？
Nǐ mǎi shénme gěi nǐ péngyǒu ？
B：________。

A：你決定去哪個大學？

你决定去哪个大学？

Nǐ juédìng qù nǎ ge dàxué ？

B：________。

2. Tasks

(1) Ask your classmates' vacation plan.

(2) Make you own plan for your vacation.

III. SUPPLEMENTARY EXPLANATION

1. One can use the "讓我 让我 ràng wǒ……" pattern, to show a more polite attitude.

IV. CULTURAL NOTES

1. New Year's Eve in Asia（亞洲地區的跨年及慶祝活動）

With the influence of Western society, people in Taiwan also celebrate Western New Year. On New Year's Eve, Taiwanese people would gather around Taipei 101, the second tallest skyscraper in the world, or local amusement parks to watch fireworks and celebrate the start of the new year. Many people would stay up the entire night either at friends' houses eating hot pot or singing at karaoke bars.

On the other hand, Northeast Asian countries, such as Japan and South Korea, celebrate this holiday in a more traditional fashion. In Seoul, South Korea, a ringing-of-bell ceremony is held at the Bosingak bell tower, where the bell would be rung thirty-three times to welcome the New Year. In Japan, however, the public is more accustomed to having family gatherings and sit in front of the T.V. to watch a singing competition called "Red and White Singing War." Early in the morning on New Year's Day, they would go to a nearby temple or shrine to pray.

2.Chinese New Year（中國新年）

Chinese New Year, also called Spring Festival, begins on December 29th and ends on January 15th (Lantern Festival) of the lunar calendar. These two weeks are liveliest and most festive time of the year. The most important day of the Spring Festival is New Year's Eve because it is the day to clean the house, worship ancestors, and hang up couplets. The greatest significance of this holiday is that families would reunite at the dinner table. Even those who live overseas will rush home to have dinner on this night. Aside from dinner, passing out red envelopes, also known as lucky money, to children after exchange of wishes is also significant as it is the most anticipated moment for the kids.

Everyone is busy on the first few days of the Spring Festival. Many people choose the first day of New Year to go to temple to worship the gods and pray for a year of peace and prosperity. On the second day, the daughters would go back to their parents' house to visit. Businesses start to open again on the fifth day. The New Year's atmosphere continues to be festive and lively until the 15th day, the Lantern Festival, when people would eat rice balls and watch beautiful lanterns as the New Year finally comes to an end.

3.Public Holidays（國定假日）

Public holidays in the U.S., China and Taiwan are a chance to get away from work for a while and spend some much needed R&R with friends and family. However, in China, big public holiday like the Spring Festival (to celebrate the Lunar New Year) have created what is known as the largest annual human migration in the world. In 2011, China's ministry of transport reported that 700 million people, more than half of China's population, made 2.85 billion road, rail, air and ferry trips to travel during the holiday season.

Often time's people are left with no choice but to buy standing tickets for buses and trains in order to go home and see their families; sometimes waiting days to finally get to their hometown. These Chinese holidays are called the "Golden Weeks," and aside from returning home many people go out and enjoy themselves in a number of ways. The result is a huge boost in China's economy, hence the nickname "Golden Week." An expression that has becoming quite popular over the years in China is "有錢沒錢回家過年" or "money or not everyone goes home for the new year."

How do you think Americans like to spend their holidays?

Vocabulary Index

	Vocabulary	Simplified Character	Pinyin	Explanation	Unit
1	啊	啊	a	a phrase final particle, indicates affirmation	4
2	吧	吧	ba	question particle indicating a request	5
3	爸爸	爸爸	bàba	(N)father	3
4	白色	白色	báisè	(N)white color	9
5	班	班	bān	(N)class	2
6	幫忙	帮忙	bāngmáng	(V)to help	12
7	比較	比较	bǐjiào	(Adv)more	9
8	餅乾	饼干	bǐnggān	(N)cookie	12
9	不錯	不错	búcuò	(SV)not bad	7
10	菜	菜	cài	(N)dish	7
11	菜單	菜单	càidān	(N)menu	7
12	餐廳	餐厅	cāntīng	(N)restaurant	7
13	廁所	厕所	cèsuǒ	(N)bathroom	6
14	常常	常常	chángcháng	(Adv)often, usually	11
15	超市	超市	chāoshì	(N)supermarket	6
16	車	车	chē	(N)car	11
17	車費	车费	chē fèi	(N)transportation fee	11
18	吃飯	吃饭	chī fàn	(V)have a meal	5
19	尺寸	尺寸	chǐcùn	(N)size	9
20	傳	传	chuán	(V)send	10

	Vocabulary	Simplified Character	Pinyin	Explanation	Unit
21	聰明	聪明	cōngmíng	(SV)smart	8
22	大概	大概	dàgài	(Adv)perhaps, most likely	10
23	蛋糕	蛋糕	dàngāo	(N)cake	5
24	但是	但是	dànshì	(Adv)but	7
25	道	道	dào	measure word for dishes	7
26	到	到	dào	(V)to go to	6
27	道地	道地	dàodì	(SV)authentic	7
28	打算	打算	dǎsuàn	(V)to plan	12
29	的	的	de	(possessive or modifying particle)	1
30	點	点	diǎn	(N)o'clock	7
31	東	东	dōng	(N, PW)east	6
32	冬天	冬天	dōngtiān	(N)winter	11
33	東西	东西	dōngxi	(N)things	6
34	都	都	dōu	(Adv)all	3
35	度假	度假	dùjià	(V)to be on a vacation	12
36	多	多	duō	(Adv)more	10
37	方便	方便	fāngbiàn	(SV)convenient	11
38	放假	放假	fàngjià	(V)to have time off	12
39	發燒	发烧	fāshāo	(V)running a fever	10
40	非常	非常	fēicháng	(Adv)very	11
41	父、母	父、母	fù、mǔ	father, mother	3

	Vocabulary	Simplified Character	Pinyin	Explanation	Unit
42	附近	附近	fùjìn	(N)nearby	6
43	父母	父母	fùmǔ	(N)parents	3
44	服務	服务	fúwù	(V)to serve	12
45	感冒	感冒	gǎnmào	(V)to catch a cold	10
46	高興	高兴	gāoxìng	(SV)happy	8
47	高興	高兴	gāoxìng	(Adj)glad	2
48	個	个	ge	measure word	3
49	給	给	gěi	(V)to give	9
50	給	给	gěi	(Prep)to	10
51	跟	跟	gēn	(P)with	11
52	公寓	公寓	gōngyù	(N)apartment	12
53	夠	够	gòu	(Adj)enough	6
54	貴	贵	guì	(SV)expensive	7
55	過	过	guò	(V)to pass	6
56	號	号	hào	(N)number	4
57	號	号	hào	(N)size number	9
58	好	好	hǎo	(Adj)good	1
59	好	好	hǎo	(Adv)so	8
60	好吃	好吃	hǎochī	(SV)delicious	7
61	好看	好看	hǎokàn	(SV)good looking	9
62	好像	好像	hǎoxiàng	(A)seems like	10

	Vocabulary	Simplified Character	Pinyin	Explanation	Unit
63	喝	喝	hē	(V)to drink	10
64	黑色	黑色	hēisè	(N)black color	9
65	很	很	hěn	(Adv)very	1
66	很少	很少	hěn shǎo	(Adv)rarely	11
67	合適	合适	héshì	(SV)appropriate	9
68	滑雪	滑雪	huáxuě	(V)ski	12
69	回	回	huí	(V)to go back	12
70	會	会	huì	(AV)be able to	2
71	或	或	huò	(Conj)or	11
72	幾	几	jǐ	(Pro)how many	3
73	家	家	jiā	(N)family	3
74	家	家	jiā	(MW)measure word for restaurants or stores	7
75	件	件	jiàn	(MW)measure word for clothes	9
76	簡訊	简讯	jiǎnxùn	(N)text message	10
77	叫	叫	jiào	(V)to call	1
78	教	教	jiāo	(V)teach	8
79	交通	交通	jiāotōng	(N)traffic	11
80	街	街	jiē	(N)street	6
81	介紹	介绍	jièshào	(V)to introduce	7
82	計畫	计画	jìhuà	(N,V)plan	12

	Vocabulary	Simplified Character	Pinyin	Explanation	Unit
83	今年	今年	jīnnián	(TW)this year	5
84	覺得	觉得	juéde	(V)to feel	9
85	決定	决定	juédìng	(V)to decide	12
86	看	看	kàn	(V)to see, to view	8
87	考慮	考虑	kǎolǜ	(V)to think about	12
88	刻	刻	kè	(N)a quarter	7
89	可愛	可爱	kěaì	(Adj)cute	3
90	可能	可能	kěnéng	(Adv)possibly	12
91	可以	可以	kěyǐ	(AV)can, may	4
92	口味	口味	kǒuwèi	(N)flavor	7
93	酷	酷	kù	(SV)cool	9
94	快要	快要	kuàiyào	(Adv)about to	12
95	辣	辣	là	(SV)spicy	7
96	來	来	lái	(V)to come	4
97	藍色	蓝色	lánsè	(N)blue	9
98	老人	老人	lǎorén	(N)older people	12
99	老師	老师	lǎoshī	(N)teacher	1
100	了	了	le	(P)particle indicating the completion of the action.	5
101	冷	冷	lěng	(SV)cold	11
102	裡面	里面	lǐ miàn	(N)inside	6
103	兩	两	liǎng	(number)two	3

	Vocabulary	Simplified Character	Pinyin	Explanation	Unit
104	練習	练习	liànxí	(V)pratice	10
105	路口	路口	lùkǒu	(N)intersection	6
106	綠色	绿色	lǜsè	(N)green	9
107	旅行	旅行	lǚxíng	(V)to travel	12
108	媽媽	妈妈	māma	(N)mother	3
109	妹妹	妹妹	mèimei	(N)younger sister	3
110	明天	明天	míngtiān	(N)tomorrow	4
111	名字	名字	míngzì	(N)name	1
112	那	那	nà	(Pro)that	4
113	那兒	那儿	nàer	(Adv)there	6
114	奶茶	奶茶	nǎichá	(N)milk tea	6
115	哪裡	哪里	nǎlǐ	(Pro)where	3
116	難	难	nán	(SV)difficult	8
117	男生	男生	nánshēng	(N)men	6
118	能	能	néng	(AV)to be able to,can	10
119	你（妳）	你（你）	nǐ(nǐ)	(P)You(singular)	1
120	你們	你们	nǐmen	(P)You (plural)	1
121	女朋友	女朋友	nǚpéngyǒu	(N)girlfriend	8
122	朋友	朋友	péngyǒu	(N)friend	1
123	便宜	便宜	piányí	(SV)cheap	11
124	漂亮	漂亮	piàoliàng	(Adv)pretty	8

	Vocabulary	Simplified Character	Pinyin	Explanation	Unit
125	平常	平常	píngcháng	(Adv)usually	11
126	請	请	qǐng	(V)to invite	4
127	親戚	亲戚	qīnqī	(N)relative	12
128	去	去	qù	(V)to go	4
129	全	全	quán	(Adv)all	7
130	讓	让	ràng	(V)to let	12
131	熱	热	rè	(SV)hot	11
132	認識	认识	rènshì	(V)to meet, to get to know	2
133	日	日	rì	(N)day	5
134	上課	上课	shàng kè	(V)to have class	10
135	上樓	上楼	shàng lóu	(V)to go upstairs	6
136	上學	上学	shàng xué	(V)to go to school	11
137	誰	谁	shéi	(Pro)who	1
138	生病	生病	shēngbìng	(SV)to be sick	10
139	生日	生日	shēngrì	(N)birthday	5
140	什麼	什么	shénme	(Pro)what	1
141	社區	小区	shèqū	(N)community service	12
142	社長	社长	shèzhǎng	(N)president/director	2
143	是	是	shì	(V)to be	1
144	適合	适合	shìhé	(SV)suitable	9
145	時候	时候	shíhòu	(N)time	5

	Vocabulary	Simplified Character	Pinyin	Explanation	Unit
146	手機	手机	shǒujī	(N)cellphone	4
147	舒服	舒服	shūfú	(SV)comfortable	10
148	水	水	shuǐ	(N)water	10
149	說	说	shuō	(V)speak	2
150	歲	岁	suì	measure word for age	5
151	他（她）	他（她）	tā /tā	(Pro)he/she	1
152	太	太	tài	(Adv)too	4
153	天	天	tiān	(N)day	4
154	天氣	天气	tiānqì	(N)weather	11
155	聽說	听说	tīngshuō	(V)hear/understand that	7
156	痛	痛	tòng	(N)ache	10
157	桶	桶	tǒng	(MW)tub	6
158	同學	同学	tóngxué	(N)classmate	2
159	桶子	桶子	tǒngzi	(N)barrel	6
160	頭	头	tóu	(N)head	10
161	往	往	wǎng	to go toward	6
162	我	我	wǒ	(P)I	1
163	我們	我们	wǒmen	(P)we	1
164	五	五	wǔ	(NU)five	3
165	下面	下面	xià miàn	(N)under	6
166	下星期	下星期	xià xīngqí	(N)next week	5

	Vocabulary	Simplified Character	Pinyin	Explanation	Unit
167	下雪	下雪	xià xuě	(V)to snow	11
168	下雨	下雨	xià yǔ	(V)to rain	11
169	想	想	xiǎng	(V)to want	4
170	夏天	夏天	xiàtiān	(N)summer	11
171	喜歡	喜欢	xǐhuān	(V)to like	2
172	新	新	xīn	(SV)new	8
173	星期	星期	xīngqí	(N)week	4
174	星期六	星期六	xīngqí liù	(N)Saturday	4
175	星期天	星期天	xīngqí tiān	(N)Sunday	4
176	洗手	洗手	xǐshǒu	(V)to wash hands	6
177	休息	休息	xiūxí	(V)to rest	10
178	選	选	xuǎn	(V)to choose	9
179	學	学	xué	(V)to learn	8
180	學生	学生	xuéshēng	(N)student	1
181	顏色	颜色	yánsè	(N)color	9
182	要	要	yào	(AV)to want to	6
183	要	要	yào	(Adv)have to	10
184	也	也	yě	(Adv)also	2
185	應該	应该	yīnggāi	(AV)should	10
186	一起	一起	yìqǐ	(Adv)together	4
187	醫生	医生	yīshēng	(N)doctor	10

	Vocabulary	Simplified Character	Pinyin	Explanation	Unit
188	一下	一下	yíxià	(N)a bit, a while	12
189	一樣	一样	yíyàng	(SV)same	11
190	有	有	yǒu	(V)There are…; to have	3
191	右邊	右边	yòu biān	(N)right side	6
192	有空	有空	yǒukòng	(V)to have free time	4
193	有名	有名	yǒumíng	(SV)famous	7
194	有趣	有趣	yǒuqù	(SV)interesting	8
195	有一點兒	有一点儿	yǒuyīdiǎnr	(Adv)a little bit	8
196	元／塊 (spoken)	元／块	yuán/ kuài	(N)dollar	9
197	月	月	yuè	(N)month	5
198	在	在	zài	to be somewhere	3
199	再	再	zài	(Adv)again	6
200	怎麼	怎么	zěnme	(QW)how	11
201	張	张	zhāng	(MW)measure word for pieces of paper	8
202	照片	照片	zhàopiàn	(N)photos	8
203	這	这	zhè	(Pro)this	2
204	眞	真	zhēn	(Adv)really	11
205	知道	知道	zhīdào	(V)know	6
206	中級	中级	zhōngjí	(Adj)intermediate level	2
207	中文	中文	Zhōngwén	(N)Mandarin	1

	Vocabulary	Simplified Character	Pinyin	Explanation	Unit
208	中午	中午	zhōngwǔ	(N)noon	7
209	周末	周末	zhōumò	(N)weekend	4
210	桌子	桌子	zhuōzi	(N)table	6
211	紫色	紫色	zǐsè	(N)purple	9
212	走	走	zǒu	(V)to walk	6
213	做	做	zuò	(V)to make	5
214	坐	坐	zuò	(V)to take	11
215	左轉	左转	zuǒ zhuǎn	(V)to turn left	6
216	做菜	做菜	zuòcài	(V)to cook	8

Terms Index

	Terms	Simplified Character	Pinyin	Explanation	Unit
1	宮保雞丁	宫保鸡丁	Gōngbǎojīdīng	Kungpao Chicken	7
2	公車	公车	gōngchē	bus	11
3	功夫	功夫	gōngfū	(N)Chinese Kungfu	2
4	加州	加州	Jiāzhōu	California	11
5	計程車	计程车	jìchéngchē	taxi	11
6	捷運／地鐵	捷运／地铁	jiéyùn/dìtiě	MRT/subway	11
7	烤肉	烤肉	kǎoròu	barbecue	4
8	跨年煙火	跨年烟火	kuànián yān huǒ	fireworks ushering in the new year	12
9	麻婆豆腐	麻婆豆腐	Mápódòufǔ	Mapuo Tofu	7
10	美國	美国	Měiguó	USA	3
11	紐約	纽约	Niǔyuē	New York	11
12	旗袍	旗袍	qípáo	cheongsam	9
13	上海	上海	Shànghǎi	Shanghai	3
14	聖誕節	圣诞节	Shèngdànjié	Christmas	12
15	四川菜	四川菜	Sìchuāncài	Sichuan cuisine	7
16	臺北	台北	Táiběi	Taipei	11
17	臺灣	台湾	Táiwān	Taiwan	3
18	唐人街	唐人街	Tángrénjiē	China Town	7
19	校車	校车	xiào chē	school bus	11

	Terms	Simplified Character	Pinyin	Explanation	Unit
20	中國菜	中国菜	Zhōngguócài	Chinese food	8
21	中秋節	中秋节	Zhōngqiūjié	Mid-Autumn Festival	4

Expressions Index

	Expressions	Simplified Character	Pinyin	Explanation	Unit
1	別擔心	别担心	biédānxīn	don't worry	6
2	不錯	不错	búcuò	not bad	2
3	大／中／小號（L, M, S）	大／中／小号	dà/zhōng/xiǎo hào	large/medium/small sizes	9
4	大家好	大家好	dàjiāhǎo	hi, everyone	1
5	當然	当然	dāngrán	of course	12
6	第一次	第一次	dì yī cì	the first time	7
7	對	对	duì	yes	3
8	對不起	对不起	duìbùqǐ	sorry	6
9	還沒	还没	háiméi	not yet	8
10	好棒	好棒	hǎo bàng	wonderful	12
11	好的	好的	hǎode	all right	10
12	很高興認識你	很高兴认识你	hěn gāoxìng rènshì nǐ	glad to meet you	2
13	很有意思	很有意思	hěnyǒuyìsi	that's very interesting	4
14	歡迎	欢迎	huānyíng	welcome	2
15	看起來	看起来	kànqǐlái	look	8
16	沒關係	没关系	méiguānxi	it's O.K.	10
17	沒問題	没问题	méiwèntí	no problem	4
18	哪裡	哪里	nǎlǐ	a humble expression to respond to a praise	2

	Expressions	Simplified Character	Pinyin	Explanation	Unit
19	你呢？	你呢？	nǐ ne	how about you?	5
20	你好	你好	nǐhǎo	hi; Hello	1
21	你們好	你们好	nǐmenhǎo	hi; Hello	1
22	請再說一次	请再说一次	qǐng zài shuō yícì	please say that again	6
23	請問	请问	qǐngwèn	excuse me	6
24	讓我考慮一下	让我考虑一下	ràng wǒ kǎolǜ yíxià	let me think about it	12
25	受不了	受不了	shòubùliǎo	unbearable	11
26	所以	所以	suǒyǐ	so	11
27	太好了	太好了	tàihǎole	wonderful	4
28	爲什麼？	为什么？	wèishénme	why?	10
29	我去過	我去过	wǒ qùguò	i have been there	7
30	謝謝	谢谢	xièxie	thank you	2
31	行啊	行啊	xíng a	yes (stress affirmative)	4
32	因爲	因为	yīnwèi	because	11
33	有的時候	有的时候	yǒudeshíhòu	sometimes	11
34	再見	再见	zàijiàn	good bye	10
35	怎麼了？	怎么了？	zěnme le	what’s up?	8
36	怎麼了？	怎么了？	zěnme le	what happened?	10
37	怎麼辦？	怎么办？	zěnmebàn	what are we going to do?	6
38	怎麼樣？	怎么样？	zěnmeyàng	what do you think?	7

	Expressions	Simplified Character	Pinyin	Explanation	Unit
39	真的（嗎）？	真的（吗）？	zhēndema	really?	12
40	真的	真的	zhēnde	really	5
41	走吧	走吧	zǒu ba	let's go	7

Supplement Explanation Index

	Vocaburary	Simplified	Pinyin	Explanation	Unit
1	八	八	bā	eight	3
2	八月	八月	Bāyuè	August	5
3	百	百	baǐ	hundred	3
4	北	北	běi	north	6
5	笨／呆	笨／呆	bèn/dāi	stupid/dumb	8
6	鼻子	鼻子	bízi	nose	10
7	醜	丑	chǒu	ugly	8
8	船	船	chuán	boat	11
9	春	春	chūn	spring	11
10	弟弟	弟弟	dìdi	younger brother	3
11	二	二	èr	two	3
12	二月	二月	Èryuè	February	5
13	耳朵	耳朵	ěrduo	ear	10
14	飛機	飞机	fēijī	airplane	11
15	分	分	fēn	minute	7
16	風	风	fēng	windy	11
17	粉紅	粉红	fěnhóng	pink	9
18	哥哥	哥哥	gēge	elder brother	3
19	紅	红	hóng	red	9
20	黃	黄	huáng	yellow	9
21	灰	灰	huī	grey	9

	Vocaburary	Simplified	Pinyin	Explanation	Unit
22	腳	脚	jiǎo	leg	10
23	機車	机车	jīchē	motorcycle	11
24	姊姊	姊姊	jiějie	elder sister	3
25	金	金	jin	golden/gold	9
26	九	九	jiǔ	nine	3
27	九月	九月	Jiǔyuè	September	5
28	苦	苦	kǔ	bitter	7
29	臉	脸	liǎn	face	10
30	零	零	líng	zero	3
31	六	六	liù	six	3
32	六月	六月	Liùyuè	June	5
33	秒	秒	miǎo	second	7
34	奶奶	奶奶	nǎinai	grandma	3
35	南	南	nán	south	6
36	七	七	qī	seven	3
37	七月	七月	Qīyuè	July	5
38	千	千	qiān	ten thousand	3
39	汽車	汽车	qìchē	car	11
40	晴	晴	qíng	sunny	11
41	秋	秋	qiū	autumn	11
42	容易 / 簡單	容易 / 简单	róngyì/jiǎndān	easy	8
43	三	三	sān	three	3

	Vocaburary	Simplified	Pinyin	Explanation	Unit
44	三月	三月	Sān yuè	March	5
45	上面	上面	shàng miàn	upside	6
46	十	十	shí	ten	3
47	十月	十月	Shíyuè	October	5
48	十二月	十二月	Shíèryuè	December	5
49	十一月	十一月	Shíyīyuè	November	5
50	手	手	shǒu	hand	10
51	四	四	sì	four	3
52	四月	四月	Sìyuè	April	5
53	四季	四季	sìjì	4 seasons	11
54	酸	酸	suān	sour	7
55	甜	甜	tián	sweet	7
56	外面	外面	wài miàn	outside	6
57	外公	外公	wàigōng	grandpa	3
58	外婆	外婆	wàipó	grandma	3
59	萬	万	wàn	million	3
60	霧	雾	wù	foggy	11
61	五月	五月	Wŭyuè	May	5
62	西	西	xī	west	6
63	夏	夏	xià	summer	11
64	鹹	咸	xían	salty	7
65	星期二	星期二	Xīngqíèr	Tuesday	4

	Vocaburary	Simplified	Pinyin	Explanation	Unit
66	星期六	星期六	Xīngqíliù	Saturday	4
67	星期三	星期三	Xīngqísān	Wednesday	4
68	星期四	星期四	Xīngqísì	Thursday	4
69	星期日	星期日	Xīngqírì	Sunday	4
70	星期五	星期五	Xīngqíwǔ	Friday	4
71	星期一	星期一	Xīngqíyī	Monday	4
72	眼睛	眼睛	yǎnjīng	eye(s)	10
73	爺爺	爷爷	yéye	grandpa	3
74	一	一	yī	one	3
75	一月	一月	Yīyuè	January	5
76	陰	阴	yīn	cloudy	11
77	雨	雨	yǔ	raining/rainy	11
78	自行車／腳踏車	自行车／脚踏车	zìxíngchē/jiǎotàchē	bicycle	11
79	棕	棕	zōng	brown	9
80	嘴巴	嘴巴	zuǐbā	mouth	10
81	左邊	左边	zuǒ biān	lest	6

國家圖書館出版品預行編目資料

青春華語 / 信世昌主編 -- 初版. -- 臺北市 : 五南, 2015.10

面；　公分

ISBN 978-957-11-8113-4（平裝）

1.漢語 2.讀本

802.86　　104007235

1X5P　華語(Chinese)

YOUTH MANDARIN TEXTBOOK I

青春華語

第一冊 (Beginning Level)

Editorial Board編輯委員（VC Chinese Team）：
Dr. Shih-chang Hsin（信世昌）、Dr. Wo-hsin Chu（朱我芯）、Dr. Dolma Ching-wei Wang（王晴薇）、Dr. Chia-ling Hsieh（謝佳玲）
Editor-in-chief主編：Shih-chang Hsin（信世昌）
Executive Editors執行編輯：Huai-xuan Chen（陳懷萱）、Chu-hua Huang（黃琡華）、Yu-hui Huang（黃郁惠）
Consultant編輯顧問：Andrew. Apolito
Dr. Laura Mei-zhi Zhang-Blust（張美智）
Assisstant編輯助理：Yun-jen Lee（李芸蓁）、Run-ting Chang（張閏婷）、Jacob Gill（高健）、Ngan-Ha Ta（謝銀河）、Calvin Chao-min Zhang（張超閔）、Irene Wu（吳艾芸）、Shih-chia Wei（魏詩珈）
Multimedia多媒體製作：Chao-hua Wang（王兆華）

Publisher（發行人）：Rong-chuan Yang（楊榮川）
Chief Editor（總編輯）：Cui-hua Wang（王翠華）
Planning Editor（企劃主編）：Hui-juan Huang（黃惠娟）
Editor（責任編輯）：Chia-ling Tsai（蔡佳伶）
Cover Design（封面設計）：Sheng-wen Huang（黃聖文）

Publisher（出版者）：Wu Nan book publishing Co.（五南圖書出版股份有限公司）
Address（地址）：4th Floor, No. 339, Sec2. Hoping East Road, Da-an District, Taipei 106, Taiwan
（臺灣106 台北市大安區和平東路二段339號4樓）
Phone（電話）：(02)2705-5066　Fax（傳真）：(02)2706-6100
Website（網址）：http://www.wunan.com.tw
E-mail（電子郵件）：wunan@wunan.com.tw
Remittance Account（劃撥帳號）：19628053
Username（戶名）：Wu Nan book publishing Co.（五南圖書出版股份有限公司）

Legal adviser（法律顧問）：Linsheng An LLP Linsheng An attorney
（林勝安律師事務所　林勝安律師）

* 本教材承蒙國科會數位典藏與數位學習華語文科技與教學國家型科技整合型計畫
【跨國合作之華語遠距協同教學模式研究－美國高中華語課程之設計與實施】
計畫編號：NSC101-2631-S-003-008-、NSC101-2631-S-003-006-）之支持完成，特此感謝。

出版日期：2015年10月初版一刷
定　　價：360元